Hiding Hearts

R. E. BRADSHAW

Other titles from R. E. Bradshaw Books

Hiding Hearts

R. E. BRADSHAW

Published by
R. E. BRADSHAW BOOKS

USA

Hiding Hearts
By R. E. Bradshaw

© **2018 by R. E. Bradshaw. All Rights Reserved.**
R. E. Bradshaw Books/March
ISBN-13: **978-0-9989549-6-7**

Website: http://www.rebradshawbooks.com
Facebook: https://www.facebook.com/rebradshawbooks
Twitter @rebradshawbooks
Blog: http://rebradshawbooks.blogspot.com
For information contact reb@rebradshawbooks.com

Acknowledgments

My father passed away before I finished this book. That loss inspired me to "get 'er done." There are at least two other books worth of notes written on this project. He read an early manuscript and wanted me to finish. Of all my writings, he liked the ones about Appletree Swamp the best. When I came home from his funeral, I pulled my big thick binder out of a box and started working on the Appletree Swamp stories again. Hiding Hearts is the first novel to come from that fount of research done so many years ago.

In that collection of notes, I followed a single Civil War soldier through his entire four years of service, down to the weather of every day, but that is another book. At the time, I was obsessed with family genealogy and the story of an ancestor who, as a young woman, was known as the "greatest horsewoman in the county." She was wild and untamed and remained so to the age of ninety-two, when she died plowing her own field.

That ancestor was my father's great aunt. I know bits and pieces of her story, but everyone knows what happens when intriguing tidbits of a tale find a writer's ear. The greatest horsewoman in the county inspired the main character of Hiding Hearts and what I hope will be a series of fiction novels that honor her legacy—that of a strong woman facing adversity with the greatest of courage. The novel takes place along the old Native American pathways and the swamps and waterways of my father's childhood. I hope he approves of how it turned out.

I send love and appreciation to all the usual suspects, but this one is for my dad.

REB

About the book…

On March 21, 1865, the mayor of Goldsborough, (now spelled Goldsboro,) North Carolina, surrendered the town to General William Tecumseh Sherman's troops. It was the end of the Union Army's march through the Confederacy, the deathblow that sealed the fate of the Southern insurrection.

Charlotte Bratcher, Lottie to friends and family, an eighteen-year-old farm girl from Wayne County, had no particular allegiance to the Southern cause. She is known as the best horse rider in the county. She and Big John, her horse, cause quite a stir, as a group of horse thieves have them both in their sights.

The Bratcher family, like most North Carolinians of the time, had no slaves and scraped a living from the land as best they could. The men in her family, conscripted into a war they did not believe in, soon lost the zeal young men have for living a war hero's tale. These Tar Heels were forced to fight in a rich man's war. By 1865, all Lottie and those like her wanted was an end to the bloodshed.

As the one hundred thousand plus Yankees spread over Wayne County like ants, Lottie and her family out in Bratcher Patch are just trying to survive. In addition to blue-coated warriors, desperate deserters, bummers, thieves, and the home patrol to deal with, Lottie is also coming to terms with a long held infatuation with Patrice Cole. Not knowing how to name her feelings for the dark-haired Miss Cole, Lottie does what she knows how to do, run. Charlotte Bratcher runs, but it's straight into the arms of the woman she has dreamed about for years.

SOME 19TH CENTURY HISTORY OF NORTH CAROLINA

"The majority of nineteenth-century North Carolinians knew neither the ostentatious gentility of the white-columned veranda nor the vivid counterculture of the "quarters" stoop. The population of the state was comprised largely of ordinary farmers, not planters and slaves. Whether white yeoman or free black, landowner or agricultural laborer, most Tar Heels lived on small farms, over two-thirds of which in 1860 were composed of a hundred acres or less. Despite the pervading influence of the plantation, rural society was built around this broad middle class...While 125,000 Tar Heels marched off to battle in service of the Confederate States of America, almost eight times that number remained at home."

— "The Way We Lived in North Carolina," Joe A. Mobley, editor, UNC Press

Dedication

Dad,
Thanks for loving my stories.
Love,
Mo

Deb,
When all is quiet,
there is always you.
Love,
Me

"In our country...one class of men makes war
and leaves another to fight it out."
—William Tecumseh Sherman

"We shall never any of us be the same as we have been."
—Sad Earth, Sweet Heaven:
The Diary of Luck Rebecca Buck

Chapter One

It Begins at the End
March 21, 1865
Goldsborough, North Carolina

"If'n y'all cain't walk, you'd better start off a crawlin'!"

The officer urged the sick and wounded men in front of him to move quickly.

"This here will be the last train outta this place and aim to be on it. Those that ain't will be left to the blue coat army comin' yonder, and may God have mercy on your miserable souls when they get here."

"Pardon me, sir, but may I inquire as to where this train is traveling?"

A wee, be-speckled man hunched over a small metal box and stared up at the Confederate soldier. The little man had a habit of crouching lower with each thunderous round of artillery explosions and then slowly rising to his tallest hunch between reports, only to duck down with every successive round. He resembled a turkey bobbing along behind the captain.

The officer barely looked at the man, as he reached out to assist a young soldier who stumbled on his crutches.

The soldier smiled up at the captain, "Thank you, sir. I'm not yet used to having just the one leg."

After righting the invalid, the soldier spat on the ground at the diminutive, box-carrying man's feet and growled out an answer to his question.

"This here train is going to Raleigh."

"Oh, that's splendid. I shall need to board at once."

"If you ain't army, you ain't getting on this here train."

"Oh dear, but the Yankees are coming. I must leave immediately with these records before they arrive. I am a representative of the state government."

"What kind of records?"

"Why tax records of course. If we don't have accurate records, how will we know who has paid and who hasn't when this mess is cleared up."

"Let me have a hold t' that box there."

The little man held out the box to which he had clung so desperately.

"Careful, now," he said. "These are the only copies."

The soldier took the box, opened the lid, and peered inside. Then without warning, he turned the box over spilling its contents into the swiftly running ditch created from weeks of seemingly endless rain that began to fall again in earnest.

"Oh, my dear sweet Jesus! What have you done?"

The little man shook with anger.

The soldier spat again, before he said, "In case you ain't looked around, these folks have paid dearly and is about to be run over by the Yankees, so I reckon you done got all you're gonna' get out of 'em."

The little man, though furious, turned and stomped back up the drive leading through the elm grove to the Borden Hotel, which at the moment was emptying wounded soldiers out as fast as they could be carried or hobble.

Lottie Bratcher had observed the entire exchange from the back of her horse. She thought the wee man lucky. He at least would be able to find a room out of this torrential rain. No matter how bloodstained, it would still be dry, which Lottie was not.

The streets of Goldsborough, North Carolina, were in a state of panic, as the town prepared to surrender to Sherman's army. Terrified children clung to their mother's skirts, as families ran behind over-burdened wagons scurrying out of town. Small eyes peeked out between window curtains until snatched away by frightened women huddled in their homes. Owners and slaves alike cowered in the shadows—unsure of what was to become of them

3

once the bluecoats arrived. Only little boys smiled, enamored of cannon fire and heroism, innocent still of the truths of war.

Refugees arrived weeks ago and had continued in a steady stream. It was a valiant, but futile attempt to outrun Sherman's forces, which were in the process of churning a forty-mile-wide scorched swath through the heart of Dixie. The parasitic mass of humanity inched through town and country, trading the precious treasures they had rescued from their abandoned or burned-out homes in exchange for food and supplies.

Most of the travelers were in search of family or friends, only to be forced to move on at every failed prospect, while Sherman's blue army set ablaze the horizon behind them. The Yankee army clawed a deep marking scar into the Confederacy, claiming it like a bear marks a tree. Sherman's troops fed the night terrors of the hungry children in its path—an imagined, but all too real fiery monster, a dragon sent only to destroy, never sleeping, always coming closer. The progress out of town had taken on a more frantic pace, as the panicked horses and people could feel the hot breath of the beast nipping at their heels. The train, the wagons, the soldiers screaming in agony, children crying, men cursing, horses rearing up, frightened farm animals loose in the streets—it all formed a deafening cacophony.

Lottie lowered the brim of her hat against the rainfall, as she moved opposite the escaping traffic, making a path for her sisters in the buckboard behind her. Trying to stay dry against the worsening shower, the two women huddled beneath a shared ratty umbrella and a gum blanket held over their shoulders, while another lay across their laps. The only things Lottie's brother, James, brought back from his short stint in the war were four gum blankets he took off some dead Yankees. He left behind half a leg in exchange.

"The Yankees give every recruit one of these blankets treated with gum rubber. Said it's to keep them dry and warm. Seems to me it gives 'em something to be wrapped in when they are wet and cold dead," James had said, with a dark-humored chuckle. He'd been that way since he came home. "So, I don't reckon they'll miss these, not as much as I'll miss the leg they took from me."

It was easy to clear a way while sitting atop Big John. He was an excellent specimen of horseflesh, black as a raven from head to hoof, except for the white star emblazoned on his broad forehead.

He stood tall at seventeen hands, towering over the fleeing masses. Lottie picked her way carefully, casting an occasional look over her shoulder to make sure her sisters followed closely.

When they reached the planned destination on the other side of the Borden Hotel, Wahl Brother's Dry Goods, Lottie stepped down from the saddle and sank ankle deep into the muddy bog that once was Center Street, the main thoroughfare through Goldsborough. Her sisters stopped just beyond the Dry Goods Store, in front of the Wahl Brother's warehouse. Two large barrels protruded from the back of the small wagon.

Lottie left Big John un-tethered at the hitching rail. He would pull the post apart if he wanted to go, so why bother. Though retaining enough untamed spirit to claim his freedom as he wished, he never left Lottie. He may wander to an apple tree or hunt up a filly, but a quick whistle brought him to her. His devotion to Lottie was matched only by her fierce love for him.

She made her way over to her sisters. Holding out her hand to the younger of the two, Martha Ann, Lottie helped her make a gentle landing in the slew at their feet.

She said to her oldest sister, "Jane, you and Martha Ann go on in. I'll watch the buckboard."

"Lottie, I've been talking to Martha Ann on the way down here, and I believe it is time you start dressing like a lady." Jane, the oldest of the six Bratcher sisters, felt compelled to continually critique her younger sister's attire. "You are eighteen, and it is time you take your place amongst the eligible girls."

Martha Ann tried to tiptoe through the mud, but finally gave up and tromped to the porch of the store, her dress pulled up over her knees.

She turned to face Lottie. "I had nothing to do with this. Jane did all the critiquing."

Jane glared at Martha Ann. "Who are you to talk, standing in public with your skirts pulled up to your ears, showing your drawers?"

"Jane, I don't know why you have to be so bad-tempered all the time."

Lottie remained silent through the entire exchange. Stepping around to the other side of the buckboard, she extended her hand to assist Jane down from the wagon.

"Look at you, acting as a gentleman offering his hand. I don't need your help."

At the exact moment Jane tried to exit the wagon on her own accord, the barrels in the back shifted. Jane flew out of the carriage headed for a face-first mud bath. Lottie prevented the full plunge, but not before Jane landed on her knees in the mucky torrent.

Martha Ann covered her mouth and said a quiet, "Oh, my."

She, like Lottie, knew better than to laugh. Jane had not been in a good mood since her husband came home from the war. Though he had been home two years and had no signs of injury, he had been discharged for poor health and wasn't fit for anything. He sat and stared off at the fields, never speaking more than ten words a day. While the rest of the family was busy trying to survive the war, John Simpson sat—wasting.

"Jane, are you all right?" Lottie lifted her big sister to her feet and brushed her hair out of her face.

Lottie stood the tallest of her sisters so far. The youngest had a shot at catching her. At the moment, she towered over the other five girls in the family, standing closer to the height of her two brothers. She was the fifth of eight siblings, a mix of wild girl and farmwoman, and at the moment, the only Bratcher family member in sight not covered in mud from the knees down.

Jane, who was trying desperately not to cry, adjusted her hat and skirts and started for the porch.

Lottie said, "I've been thinking too, about the way I dress. I saved this silver coin for material, but Ma's not up to sewing, so a new store bought dress will do." Knowing pity or charity would only make Jane angrier, she pulled a coin from her pocket and held it out to her. "You take this on in the store and get a new dress to wear home, and then I'll take it back from you when you're done with it."

Jane stopped and stood still for a moment. She then turned to Lottie.

"God made no sweeter child than you, Lottie Bratcher. You got the gift, child. You can always make me smile."

She stood on her toes and kissed Lottie lightly on the cheek.

As they turned to go, Lottie called after her two sisters, "Tell him Ma will not be making another batch anytime soon, so you'll be needing a good price for the barrels. That's the sweetest wine in the county. The Yankees will buy it—or steal it."

The last part was said under her breath, as Jane and Martha Ann had not waited for her to finish before entering the store.

Lottie pulled a gum blanket from the buckboard and threw it over Big John's back to cover her saddle, as the deluge grew stronger.

"Sorry, big fella, but I don't reckon they'd take too kindly to a horse on the porch."

A moment later four large black men came out to the wagon and removed the barrels, taking them back into the warehouse. Lottie nodded at them, and they nodded back, the way familiar people do.

She had lived among black folks all her life. Not as the people who had slaves to do their bidding, but among and with Negroes who scraped a living from the soil just like she did. The slaves Lottie knew of lived on the few plantations around Wayne County. She neither owned slaves nor knew a Bratcher that ever purchased one. In fact, her mother's family tree contained a strong Quaker lineage and a French-Haitian great-grandmother, brought to America as a slave.

Lottie was the child of a rich man's mistress, considered just a notch above the black freedmen in the social structure of the South. Since Lottie knew blood ran the same color, no matter the pigment of skin that held it in, she treated everyone the same. Besides, the way men behaved in previous centuries, while colonizing this part of Carolina, there wasn't as much pure Caucasian blood as the aristocrats liked to think. That one-drop rule—a single drop of sub-Saharan-African blood makes one a Negro—would fail a lot of folks, truth be known.

Lottie removed her hat and shook out the long, dark-blonde ringlets trapped inside. Her grandmother claimed that Lottie, of all the female relatives, looked most like her French-Haitian great-grandmother.

"That hair will never be tamed," she would say, while laughing at Lottie's attempts to straighten it.

She held the hat by the brim between her front teeth, while she re-bundled the mass of hair. She then replaced the planter's hat atop her head and stuffed the curls inside. To anyone looking,

Lottie appeared a tall, thin young man clad in a full-length oil coat, trousers, and riding boots. At five-feet-seven-inches tall, Lottie could pass for a boy from a distance, but up close her fine features gave her femininity away. Piercing hazel eyes looked out from under the brim of her hat. Perfectly plump lips clasped a thin piece of pine in one corner.

While checking to see that she was unobserved, Lottie pulled a small tin from her inside breast pocket. Taking the stick from her mouth she dipped it into the can, bringing it out again with a tiny dip of snuff, which she quickly tucked inside her lip. Putting the stick back in her mouth, she replaced the lid on the tin and hid it away. Snuff was a hot commodity. No one need know she had it.

Looking in through the store window, Lottie could see Martha Ann holding up a dress in front of Jane. The store looked almost cleared of stock. There seemed to be only two choices for the dress, both made out of feed sack patterns. Lottie enjoyed watching her older sisters act like young women again. Jane was twenty-two, old before her time and Martha Ann was just turning twenty. The war had aged them all.

Martha Ann married Avery May last September, when they were both 19. Avery, a gentle boy, had avoided serving in the army because of childhood asthma, but by 1864, physical ability was less a criterion than before. Avery slipped out two days after his wedding night, enlisted in Company D with Lottie's brother Jefferson, and promptly went missing twenty-two days later at Cedar Creek.

One of the men who had carried in the barrels drew Lottie's attention to the side door, where he spoke to Mr. Wahl, who then turned and called out to Jane. Jane's brow creased with concern during the conversation with Mr. Wahl. She then smiled and looked down at the silver in her hand. Jane turned to Martha Ann and spoke. Martha Ann quickly put the dresses back and followed Jane over to the counter, where she pulled a short list out of her purse. The clerks set about filling the order as Jane asked to be excused to wash-up in the back room.

Mr. Wahl motioned Martha Ann closer to the counter and began an intense conversation. Lottie wondered what they could be talking about. Martha Ann had some strange things to say these days, which worried Lottie. Just as she was about to go in, Martha

Ann kissed the old man on the cheek, ran to the dresses, picked one, and rushed to the back room grinning like a happy school girl. Mr. Wahl laughed and turned toward the storefront. Seeing Lottie, he waved. She smiled and waved back. It was nice to see impending doom had not jaded everyone.

It was the change in Mr. Wahl's expression that first alerted Lottie that something was wrong. She turned around just in time to see four refugees step up on the porch.

"What we got here, boys? Look at that purty thing under that hat," the tallest one said.

He appeared to be the leader. The whole lot looked like they had been rolling in the mud for days. Matted clods of red clay and black swamp mud clung to their hair and clothes. Not one of them had pants legs below the knee, and only two had rags tied on their feet for shoes. The rest had bare feet caked with muck and blood. The oldest was probably fifteen and the youngest about ten. The accent betrayed their South Carolina low country roots.

The boy reached out and took Lottie's hat, causing her curls to bounce down to her shoulders. He placed the hat on his head and leered at her.

"Damn, look at that," one of the others said.

Big John snorted and stamped, drawing the young ruffians' attention away from Lottie. She reached under her slicker for the Colt Navy 1851, .36 caliber pistol, foraged off the battlefield when the Yankees first came in '62. The name had nothing to do with it being Navy issue, but referenced a Texas naval battle engraved on the cylinder. Lottie kept the pistol tucked in the belt at her waist for just these occasions, when being a woman meant fighting for every inch of ground. Lottie cocked the trigger back and stuck the end of the barrel in the big one's ear before he could turn around.

"If you would be so kind, I'd like my hat back."

The boy froze, but his mates didn't. One of them made the mistake of ripping off the gum blanket and hopping on Big John's back. The horse was so tall; the boy could only make it onto the saddle with his stomach. In this position, his head hung off one side, and his feet swung wildly on the other. Lottie broke into a smile.

Big John swung his head around and looked the flailing boy directly in the eyes. This induced cries of anguish from the young chap. Just then one of his friends tried to boost him up from the other side. Big John whipped his head around and frightened the friend, who slipped on the discarded gum blanket and fell back in the mud. He then crawled backward until he was able to gain solid ground and his balance. He got to his feet and ran into the crowd.

The terror-stricken boy on Big John's back let out a howl, as the horse lowered his haunches. In a flash, the boy was sailing through the air. He came down on a cart in the middle of Center Street. The owner of said cart commenced beating the boy, as the caravan continued its slow progress down the street.

Left alone now and reduced to a sniffling child, the once proud young hooligan could hold his water no more. Lottie looked down at the trickle of liquid trailing down the boy's leg.

"Lord have mercy, boy. Did you lose your manhood?"

"Now, Lottie, no harm has been done. Why don't you let the young man apologize and move on? And boy," Mr. Wahl turned to the young man, "don't you come into Wayne County starting any trouble. You best be moving on."

"No, sir. I mean, yes, sir. Sorry 'bout the trouble ma'am. Here's your hat."

Lottie lowered the pistol. She slid the weapon back into the belt at her waist and then reached out to take the hat from the trembling boy. He turned and had only made one step when he felt the toe of Lottie's boot catch him in the hind end. He learned to fly, swim, and crawl before he made it out of sight.

"Get your tail out of Wayne County, you South Carolina trash."

"That might be good advice for most folks today," Mr. Wahl said, as he stepped up beside her.

"Good-morning, Mr. Wahl. Sorry about the disturbance. Looks like the wounded are pouring in from Bentonville. What have you heard?"

"From what I gathered at the hospital this morning, it looks like Uncle Billy intends to have Goldsborough. The two railroads meeting here make it valuable real estate. Bentonville is a lost cause, and Johnston is pulling back to Smithfield. There's some rebel cavalry waiting in Webbtown south of here, some home guard too, but it's just a matter of time. The Yankees already got 'em a pontoon crossing at Cox's Bridge. Sherman, Schofield, and Terry are coming some ninety thousand strong, and no one is going to stop them. That's the last of Bragg's troops there, loading onto those flat cars."

Lottie spat a long stream of snuff juice out into the street.

"Charlotte Bratcher, your manners," Jane said, as she exited the store. She had not seen or heard any of the previous events.

Mr. Wahl gave a knowing wink to Lottie and addressed Jane.

"Why that dress looks marvelous on you. It is a shame you must travel in this weather."

"Thank you, Mr. Wahl," replied Jane, as she swept her muddy cape aside to reveal the new dress. She had obviously tried to clean the cape only to make matters worse. "Your generosity is most kind. Could you have a porter gather my soiled dress and wrap it for the trip home? I do hope I can salvage it. It being practically ruined and all."

Martha poked Jane in the ribs. "You do put on airs at times."

"I will have your supplies brought out to your wagon. And now if our business is concluded, I have to get things in order. After all, the Yankees will be here soon, and my brother and I have stores that need tending. Good morning ladies. God be with you."

"And with you and yours," Martha Ann and Jane said in unison. Lottie simply tipped her hat.

Once loaded, the sisters turned the wagon toward home and attempted to stay out of the way of the frenzied swarm, as they waited near the front of the Gregory Hotel, now converted to a hospital. The throng of anxious people escaping north through town was made even more so by the sight of Confederate cavalry fleeing on lathered horseback.

The rain let up some, but persisted in a drizzle. The wounded had arrived all day from Bentonville, and now they were coming in from as close as Everittsville. The booming of the cannons had grown steadily closer as the day progressed. Retreating Confederate troops added to the portended terror of the inevitable Yankee occupation.

General Bragg had left days ago, leaving a small force to defend Goldsborough. He held up Yankee General Schofield's right corps, led by Cox, for a week in Kinston. He burned the bridges and then retreated to assist Johnston's defenses concentrated near Smithfield on the corridor to Raleigh. The fighting had been heavy around Bentonville and Cox's Bridge to the west for the past three days, with sporadic fighting to the south as Schofield's advance party zeroed in on Goldsborough, an important hub on the eastern seaboard railroads.

Cotton had been removed from warehouses and placed in the median of Center Street. The bales had been set afire. Instead of burning, the rain-soaked bundles smoldered and filled the air with gray smoke and ashes. Women and children busied themselves moving cotton bales inside their homes to line the walls, hopefully preventing bullets from reaching those inside. Young boys hung out of upper floor windows in the hotel, hopeful of catching a glimpse of the bloodshed.

It was hoped that Sherman would not burn Goldsborough. His butchery in North Carolina had not been as horrendous as what he had done in Georgia and South Carolina. Sherman's reluctance to blaze his path as before may have been in part due to the growing numbers of Union loyalists and anti-war Copperheads in the old North state.

Sherman targeted government buildings and arsenals, while only his bummers, men who foraged for supplies for the Union army, scavenged through the countryside. The fires still burned, atrocities still occurred, and the land was still stripped of all things an army could need or want, but it wasn't nearly the damage done deeper in the southern states. The refugees told stories of Sherman's wagon train of bummers overburdened with supplies while the southerners starved in front of them. Men with chickens and hams slung over their shoulders marched with Sherman's army into the ol' North state, and still they took more from people who already had nothing.

An errant cannon ball crashed through the pines on the southern edge of town below the Big Ditch, a stream that bordered the east and south of town. The pine trees snapped and exploded with such force it shook the windows in the hotel. A particularly sharp report of artillery thundered across the sky. The old mule, Jake, attached to the buckboard was startled into action. Martha Ann pulled sharply on the reins.

"It's okay, Jake. We have nothing to worry about."

"Nothing to worry about? Martha Ann where do you get these ideas of yours? Of course we have to worry. We are sitting here like fish in a barrel. The Yankees are just down the road, and you say we have nothing to worry about." Jane's momentarily pleasant mood had disappeared.

"I can't tell you how I know. It's a secret."

Lottie looked down at her sister from atop the giant horse. What could Martha Ann know? Lottie had been extra careful to keep her affairs clandestine.

"We don't keep secrets, right Jane? Tell us what you know, Martha Ann."

"All right, but you must swear not to breathe a word to a soul. Someone may get hurt."

Alarmed, Lottie jumped down from Big John and drew closer to the wagon. Should anyone be listening, she wanted nothing said too loudly.

"Well, you know Aunt June over at Papa's place? Before she left, Aunt June conjured up Avery for me and said he was coming home. He's just lost. He wasn't gone long enough to be dead. And she said that Jefferson was coming home all in one piece. She said the war would be over soon and all would go back to the way it was when life was sweet."

"Oh hell, Martha Ann," Lottie spat. "That ol' woman filled your head with nonsense and don't call that man Papa around me."

Lottie saw the hurt in Martha Ann's eyes before the words had finished streaming from her mouth. She reached out and touched Martha Ann under the chin, turning her face up to hers.

"I apologize. I don't know what's gotten into me. Of course, Avery is coming home and Jeff too. You go on believing for all of us."

"I know what's wrong with you," said Jane. "It's those trousers you insist on wearing."

"Just shut up, Jane. Leave Lottie alone. You make more fuss than a wet settin' hen."

"You encourage her. Tell her it is not proper. No man will have her."

"Hush up you ol' bitty. You have a man and what is he worth?"

Jane was too angry to respond verbally, but her hand was lightning quick. She swung straight for Martha Ann's cheek. Lottie grabbed Jane's wrist before contact was made.

"Well now, there are the sisters I know and love, behaving as usual. I thought I told you to watch these two, Lott."

It was the voice of James Edwards, older brother to Jane by eleven years. He was given his father's name, though he too was illegitimate. Their father had claimed both boys in the family, but the girls remained without his name. James limped toward the wagon with the aid of a crutch. He carried several newspapers under his other arm.

"Brother, 'tis a full-time job." Lottie released Jane's arm. "What's the news?"

"The Yankee's are comin'," he grinned.

James Edwards had fought in the home guard in 1862 the last time the Yankees came to town. He had been shot in the leg, but had not left the field. One of his friends was in the process of drowning, shot while crossing the river, so James went in after him. He took two more bullets, one that shattered his knee. He recovered his friend only to have him die in his arms on the shore.

A Yankee doctor took James's leg and then he was released to return home, with the promise to not take up arms again. He told that story often, commenting that if the Yankees made a one-legged man swear to refrain from warfare, they must indeed be afraid of the southern warrior.

Even as he kept up the façade of rebel bravado, in private, the well-read James confided to Lottie long ago, "The south can never win this war. It is a war for the soul of a nation. The Union must persevere."

James Edwards was a one-legged, dark-humored, widower, father of two, and a happy man. The kind of contentment a man finds after he has faced life's worst challenges and survived certain death.

He would smile and say to doubters of the authenticity of his joviality, "I've already had the worst days of my life."

"Well, if the Yankees are coming, you better get a move on," Lottie said, as James lifted himself onto the bench seat of the buckboard.

He amazed her with his upper body strength and the agility he'd accomplished in the three years since losing the leg. James wanted a prosthetic leg, but that cost money and the demand was high, which drove prices even higher. Lottie hoped when the war was over, she would be able to make enough money to buy him one.

Once seated, James replied, "I'll see to it that these two don't kill each other before we get home. You hurry up with the visit to Doc and come on home as soon as you can. Be careful, sister."

Lottie grabbed the horn and the back of the saddle, hooked a toe in a stirrup, and bounded up onto Big John with a hop, which was an athletic maneuver of some achievement.

"I'll be there before supper is on the table."

Chapter Two

Babes at War

Heading east on Walnut, Lottie passed more wagons loaded with wounded soldiers moving west toward the train station. There were bloody stumps protruding everywhere. The stink of rotting flesh hung in the air. Turkey buzzards circled overhead.

Lottie whispered under her breath, "So many lives wasted for nothing."

Cots with wounded were shuttled by orderlies, while the less injured walked and hobbled along the street. These soldiers would be well enough to head back into battle soon. Lottie wondered how many of them would survive another trip to hell.

"Hey, pretty lady, those trousers don't cover that beauty. Give us a smile," a soldier in the back of a wagon yelled out.

Lottie smiled at the young man and watched as his face lit up.

"You boys come on back to see us when the war is over."

The men in the wagon teased the young man. One let out a rebel yell, as he doffed his hat and bowed at the waist. It was only then that Lottie realized he had no legs.

"Lordy, will this war never end?"

On the north side of the street, in the old Chinquapin grove, the county courthouse rose into view. A source of great pride for the self-important men who ran Wayne County, Greek columns framed the ten-year-old red brick and stone structure. Refugees seeking help from a falling government crowded overloaded wagons in next to the buggies of prominent citizens. Lottie recognized Jack Cole standing at the top of the steps surrounded by men from the county. Cole involved in the goings on within the courthouse could only mean trouble.

At the corner of Walnut and William Streets, Lottie turned north toward the tallest building in town, Wayne Female College. The bell tower on top of the four-story, red brick building could be seen above all other structures in Goldsborough. Lottie remembered coming into town as a girl and watching the tower go up in 1854. It was a wonder to behold. It was still the tallest single thing she had ever seen.

On the front of the college facing William Street, two opposing staircases were joined at the top by a portico. The entryway opened into the second-floor foyer. The railings and steps were splashed with blood. Out of all the exits came the treated soldiers to be placed under tents serving as makeshift recovery rooms. Up the steps went more wounded, new arrivals from the battlefields.

Black porters bore the bloodied and battered men in and out of the hospital with the walking-wounded helping where they could. Young women scurried about holding a hand here, dabbing a fevered brow there. Older women mopped bloody floors and changed bandages. On one side of the lawn, black women stood over cast iron kettles stirring boiling sheets. Now that the sun was beginning to peek through the clouds, bloodstained sheets were being hung out to dry.

"Men make bloody messes women have to clean up," Lottie's mother had said once. In the last four years, Lottie had come to understand what she meant.

Dismounting by the picket fence that surrounded the property, she gazed south over the fields filled with wounded and retreating men. In among the soldiers, fleeing citizens flooded north, desperately running ahead of Sherman's armies. The sight quickened Lottie's heartbeat.

"I will not dally, Big John." She rubbed a hand on his neck and gave him a pat. "We must be getting home, too."

The horse's velvet soft lips brushed Lottie's shoulder. He snorted nervously and stamped a front hoof. Lottie felt the uneasiness too.

"Be mindful," she said to Big John as if he knew her intent. Lottie believed he did, and that was enough. She tossed his reins over the fence and headed up the walkway.

"That horse ain't gonna be there when you come back," a soldier stretched out on a makeshift gurney called out to her.

"If they can mount him, they can have him," Lottie said, following the warning with her unusually wicked grin. "You might want to stick around to watch."

The soldier gave a nod of understanding. He stared back at the massive black horse, seeming to imagine what a stud like that could do to a man he didn't want on his back. As Lottie watched, two porters scooped up the soldier and carried him to a waiting wagon. He had no legs.

"Sorry, I'm going to miss the show," he said, waving his cap at Lottie. "I've a train to catch."

"Godspeed, good sir," Lottie called back. It was a weak offering for a young man who lost so much but remained kind. That was unequivocally heroic in Lottie's estimation.

When Lottie reached the stairs, she did not go up but entered the lower right door on the first floor. As her hand reached the handle, she heard the bells of the courthouse begin to ring, followed by the carillons of every church in town. The alarm rose from the bell tower of the building she was about to enter, adding anxiousness to the already distressed citizens.

"Yes, boys," Lottie said, with sarcasm born of contempt for male enthusiasm for war and all its trimmings. "The Yankees are coming." A loud boom shook the building, as someone fired the cannon in the courthouse square. "In fact, I believe they are here."

Lottie ducked inside and instantly gagged. The odor of death and rot overwhelmed her. She used the wall to steady herself.

A porter carried a bucket full of bloody rags, spilling the tainted water behind him.

As he passed, he said, "Put a kerchief over your nose until you get used to it. It'll help."

Lottie pulled a red bandana out of her pocket and held it to her nose with one hand, swatting at flies with the other. Along with the smell were the sounds—clanging pans, screaming, crying, moaning, begging, raised voices of the staff as they tried to get men out of the hospital and treat the new wounded coming in. The worst sights

18

were the children. Cannon fire and minié balls did not distinguish between combatants and the innocent. A small girl, only two or three years old, sobbed silently against her mother's chest—the bloody bandage on her amputated arm in stark contrast to her nearly white blonde hair.

Lottie lowered the bandana, not wanting the child to see her revulsion. She searched her pocket for a piece of the rock candy her family made before supplies dwindled to nothing. The sugar crystals formed on a string soaked in sugar water with a little vinegar. They used Apple Brandy for flavoring. It was a great treat, especially in these times when sugar was so scarce.

"Here little one, something sweet for you to suck on."

The little girl took a weak breath and sighed heavily. Lottie placed the candy in the little girl's remaining hand. Her tiny fingers clasped around the treat before her drooping eyelids closed again. Lottie brushed the hair from the child's forehead with her fingertips. The girl's skin was sticky with fever. The mother silently smiled up at Lottie. She wasn't much older in years, but the war had drawn deep lines of worry on her brow.

"I pray the pain leaves soon," Lottie said, wishing it for both the child and the mother.

Moving away Lottie reached the main hall where she saw cots end-to-end, running the length of the building, every bed occupied. Lottie saw Dr. William Davis making his way through the sea of broken men. Some reached out to him crying in pain. Others, too weak to make sounds, followed him with hollow eyes.

Dr. Davis's apron was streaked with blood. Crimson droplets speckled the top layer of his white hair. He stepped into a room at the end of the hall, set up as an operating room. Porters were mopping as fast as they could, but would never catch up. Lottie felt her stomach turn over as she saw the doctor reach for a saw. The man on the table began to shriek and beg, before a copper cup was placed over his face. Lottie walked toward the other end of the hall, putting distance between her and what was to come next.

"Lott Bratcher, I do declare."

Lottie looked down at one of the cots lining the hallway to see a familiar face, but she couldn't quite place him.

She replied, "Well, hello handsome."

She drew closer to the smiling face. Sadness washed over her with the realization that it was a boy she had known all her life. When he left for the war, he weighed more than 200 pounds. Now he lay in this festering hallway in a makeshift hospital with bones showing and sunken features, barely recognizable.

"You sure are a sight fer sore eyes. I just got here from Richmond on the last train, and you're the first person I seen that I knowed for sure, ceptin' Doc. I been gone awhile, but I'd never forget those eyes."

"William Bailey, you haven't lost your charm. What's ailin' ya'? Are you shot through?"

"No, I been shot at enough, though. I got the bloody flux, the Tennessee Trots they tell me. Cain't seem to get over it. Been down in the bed for I don't know how long. They sent me home to my momma, 'cause they cain't make it stop. Maybe she can."

"Does your momma know you're here?"

"I sent word soon as I got here and they's supposed to be comin' with the wagon. My bad luck to get home just before the Yankees come."

"Well, you are home, so don't you worry none about those Yankees."

"I seen them bluecoats do some terrible things. I seen our boys do some worse. The war changed some folks for the better, but evil hooked a good number of 'em. You stay clear of that sort, ya' hear?"

Lottie patted his bony shoulder and looked back down the hall. Dr. Davis headed her way, wiping his hand on a bloody towel handed to him by one of the dressers. His steps were quick, and he gave out orders as he hurried on his way, occasionally stopping to give comfort to a wounded man. Dr. Davis had birthed some of these young men. The madness of it all was more than he could bear. He had told Lottie on one of her recent visits that if he stopped to think about the butchery, it would kill him. He had to keep moving and save the ones he could.

"It's good to see you are home, Will. I know your family will take very good care of you. I'll come see you once you get settled in at home."

Lottie turned and moved toward Dr. Davis. He saw her before she reached him and a broad smile filled his face.

20

"A vision of loveliness in this dungeon of doom."

"Doc, you are a marvel. Ma always says you have a special place in heaven, and after what I've seen today, I have a mind to believe her."

"As long as these idiots insist on fighting this war, I will do my duty by these poor souls. When this is over, I think I'll quit medicine altogether and take up farming."

"You'll never quit, Doc. What would Ma do without you?"

"Speaking of your mother, seeing as you are here, it must mean she is down with the sick head again."

"She took down a couple of days ago. I tried the herbs you suggested, but she swears your cure is all that works." Lottie leaned in close for the next part. "That wound on her leg isn't any better either."

Doc had already pulled a small scrap of paper and the stub of a lead pencil from his pocket. He began writing before Lottie finished speaking. He raised an eyebrow at the wounded leg part but said nothing. When he finished writing, Doc tucked the stub of lead back in his pocket and handed the paper to Lottie.

"Take this up to the next floor. Go down to the room at the north end of the hall. Mary will fill this for you. I've asked for more than you'll need. Save what you don't use for another time. I don't know what will happen when the Yankees get here, but I do know they will take over this hospital and everything in it. And Lottie, you have to keep that leg wound clean and dry. Change the bandages regularly. Mary will give you some to take with you. If it starts rotting, you'll have to bring her in."

"God bless you, Doc. Until we meet again." She pecked him on the cheek.

"Hold on, child. You've smeared some blood on you. I'm sorry. I seem to have a fine mist of it on me everywhere."

Dr. Davis pulled out his handkerchief and dabbed her cheek. When he made eye contact, Lottie saw his deep sadness.

"You be careful, Miss Lottie Bratcher. When this is over, I plan to claim a dance with you."

"Your claim will be granted."

He smiled once more before striding down the hall, keeping a brave face in the midst of such suffering.

21

Lottie climbed the stairs and found Mary in a small room. The walls were lined with shelves filled with all nature of herbs and cures. Since the blockade had been successful, medicines were difficult if not impossible to obtain. Doc depended on the old country wisdom of the slave women, who gathered and prepared most of the cures found in this room.

Mary was a short round black woman around fifty-years-old. Folks called her Medicine Woman or Medicine Mary, in honor of her encyclopedic knowledge of natural cures. She had been with Doc for thirty years. Nobody knew where she came from, and she and Doc weren't telling. He treated her more like family than a slave. Their personal arrangement was a mystery, which added to the Medicine Woman's lore.

Mary hummed as she worked at a small table in the middle of the room. She crushed leaves with a pestle. Her strong hands only stopped their mission when the bell tower again began its frantic clanging.

"Lawd, have mercy. Them bells goin' t' make me crazy. White folks don't need no bells to tell 'em dem Yankees is comin'. Cain't they hear dem cannons yonder?"

"Mary, you are not far from right on that one."

"Lawd, Lottie Bratcher, y'all is growed to be a woman, sure as ya' born'd. H'ain't seen y'all folks in a spell."

"Ma come down with the sick head again. I got this scrap a paper from Doc."

Dr. Davis had violated the law and taught Mary to read. He swore she could be a medical doctor. He told all that would listen that he'd learned more from Mary than he did in the medical department at Chapel Hill. Mary took the note and headed for the wall of jars by the window.

"Yes ma'am, this here'll move that devil headache right on. And when we done here, y'all best be gettin'. We got wounded from just outside Webbtown now. Yankees is close enough to spit through da door."

"I intend to do just that."

"What's this here? Somebody got a woun' won't heal?"

"Ma fell on the hoe in the garden. Just won't close."

Mary gazed at Lottie.

22

"Girl, I done knowed y'all since you was born'd an I knows when I been lied to."

"Mary, I can't tell you the truth. You're better off not knowin'."

"You right. I don't need to know particulars. Jus' tell me, is it a shot-ball hole? Cause them kinds o' holes an' hoe holes needs different cures."

Lottie thought for a minute and answered that it was a shot ball hole. She begged Mary to keep the knowledge confidential, which Mary took as an insult for being asked.

"Chil', I know so many secrets on folks aroun' here, if I was to tell what I know'd the whole county'd be in a commotion. Secrets is safe with Mary."

Lottie thanked Mary and made her way to where she had left Big John. Several refugees were standing near him, apparently deciding what to do next. His reins hung down on the ground in front of him. His head was high, showing the whites of his eyes, nostrils flared. Big John was ready to pummel the next one that moved. As Lottie grew closer, she saw that one man was already down behind the horse. She approached and with a single pat on his withers settled her big man down.

"Shhh, it's okay."

She began placing the jars and bandages in the saddlebags.

The man on the ground yelled up to her, "Ya' ain't goin' t' get on that beast is ya'? He's a man killer!"

"Only men who try to steal him," Lottie said, as she grinned at the man, dipped the brim of her hat in his direction, and grabbed the reins.

She tapped Big John on the shoulder, at which point he knelt on one knee. Lottie grabbed the saddle horn and tucked a toe in the stirrup. She clucked to Big John who righted himself, the momentum gracefully sweeping Lottie up with him and into the saddle. The horse then snorted at the men who had tried unsuccessfully to mount him.

The man on the ground got up slowly, rubbing his backside. Lottie heard him say, "Well, I'll be hog-swallered," as she rode away down William Street.

Chapter Three

The Powers That Be

Lottie patted Big John on the neck, as they turned back up Walnut Street. He snorted his approval and pranced even prouder with his head held high. He was looking around, taking in the sights, secure amidst the madness with his girl in the saddle.

They arrived at the Wayne County Courthouse just in time to see the last of the menfolk trailing inside. She found a good spot under an elm tree and left Big John to nibble on some grass. On the way in Lottie repositioned her hat, shoved her hair up inside, and pulled the brim down lower. She moved toward the side door, a less conspicuous entrance.

Squinting at the now fully exposed sun, Lottie calculated it must be near noon. She needed something to eat. Her last meal came before sunrise when they set off from home. The cornbread and cup of sweet potato coffee had burned off long ago, but things were more important at the moment.

The door creaked as Lottie slowly slid it open. She stopped, listened for sounds, and discovering none opened the door just wide enough to slip in and close it behind her. The creaking was louder on the closing. Sure that someone had heard the commotion, she hurried across the hall to the central staircase.

Lottie hopped up the three steps to the landing, turned right to ascend the next flight of stairs, and ran headlong into Patrice Henriette Cole. The collision knocked Lottie's hat brim down over her face. Even without being able to see who impeded her progress, Lottie would know that fragrance anywhere.

Patrice Cole would typically stand eye to eye with the young woman whose hat and face remained smashed into her chest, but as she was on a higher step, her breasts were eye level with Lottie's nose. Lottie caught herself taking Patrice in with a deep breath. She smelled like roses.

Patrice Cole had been an infatuation of Lottie's since childhood. She had spent her youth watching Patrice's thick, completely straight, coal-black hair shimmer in the sun from a distance, never too close. Close meant Lottie might have to talk to the always-friendly Patrice. Talking meant Lottie had to look into Patrice's soft brown doe-eyes, which was to be avoided.

When Patrice turned sixteen, she and her twin brother were sent up north to be schooled but returned each year for summer breaks and winter holidays. Lottie had been able to keep abreast of Patrice's blossoming womanhood. After it was clear the war was not going to end, the twins had returned home a little over a year ago. So far, Lottie had avoided having to speak directly to Patrice. She could not explain the yearning she felt for the dark-haired girl in her dreams, and for that very reason, Lottie Bratcher hated Patrice Cole.

"Whoa there. What's your hurry?"

Patrice smiled down at Lottie, a position they were rarely in. The perspective sent a disarming charge of unknown origin through Lottie's chest. The glowing, as Lottie came to call it, crept downward, deep where it shouldn't.

Lottie jumped back and looked away, saying, "Sweet Jesus, do you enjoy scaring the life outta folks?"

"Lottie Bratcher, you've never been afraid a day in your life." Patrice chuckled, and the glow became an inferno. "What in God's name are you doing here? Don't you know the Yankees are on the edge of town?"

Lottie fought the blush, which seemed to make it worse. She tried to brush past her nemesis, saying, "If it's any business of yours, I came to get Ma's cure from the doctor."

Patrice blocked her path, playfully. "Well, this isn't a hospital, and you're sneaking into the courthouse, so that isn't all you're up to."

25

Lottie took a step back down the stairs. She required space from those eyes, the smile, and the scent of roses. She looked down at the hat she mindlessly turned in her hands.

"I saw all the menfolk coming in, and I thought I'd see what the powers that be have to say."

Patrice was happy to play informant. "They are up there with Mayor Privett. He's going to ride out with a flag of truce and surrender the town. He says that's the only way to keep them from burning us out."

"What does ol' Jack think about the plan?"

"Papa says it's worth a try."

Lottie shook her head. "That doesn't sound like Jack. He's usually running the show or trying to stop the one that is."

Patrice smiled. "You know him well. Papa and my younger, blood-crazed, half-brother are busy organizing patrols to ride the county. He's heard about how the Yankees have colored troops carrying real rifles. He is not about to have a black soldier with a gun terrorizing the women in these parts."

"It isn't blue-coated black soldiers that we worry about at home. There's plenty enough trouble without looking for more."

"I didn't say I thought it was a good idea," Patrice said. "Although, the bummers with the Union army will come too, and you may end up being glad Papa is so willing to serve. He swears we have to arm ourselves and begin guerrilla war like they have out in Kansas." Patrice performed an exaggerated impression of her father, "There'll be no bumming in Wayne County, if Jack Cole has anything to do with it."

Patrice grinned at her audience of one, waiting for the reception. Lottie thought she did a fair job of mocking Jack and nearly smiled. Enjoying Patrice's company made Lottie uncomfortable, which made her angry.

She lashed out. "So all the boys who bought their way out of this war and the old men too feeble to serve, along with a few broken down soldiers are going to protect me and mine?" Lottie let out a contemptuous laugh. "I'll keep my pistol close if you don't mind. There isn't a rich man in this county who will stick his neck out for us poor folks."

"We're all poor folks now, Lottie. We have to stick together."

"What do you know about poor? You have on shiny new shoes. You have food and shelter. You are wearing what appears to be a new suit, and you did not have to lift a finger to make any of that happen."

"This war has changed people, Lottie. We're not so different, you and I. The slaves have mostly run off the Cole place. The ones that stayed are eating out of the pot with the ones they are serving. The money Jack has is worthless Confederate paper money. Look at my hands. I've been working the fields some, and doing duty at the hospital."

"May the Lord strike me dead, Patrice Cole has dirt under her nails. She's human after all."

"You don't have to be so mean, Charlotte Bratcher. I was never mean to you like the other girls. We're all going to need one another soon. When the war is over, and we have only our friends to depend on, I hope you'll count me as one. Besides, I've found that I like having my hands in the soil."

Lottie was unmoved by Patrice's plea. "It's a novelty. It will wear off."

"I don't think so, Lottie. I've spent this war volunteering at hospitals on both sides of the Mason-Dixon line. I see those broken men in my sleep. I want this war to end, but I'm afraid nothing will ever be the same. I, myself, am forever changed."

Lottie noted the sadness in Patrice's expression. For a brief second, she felt a tinge of something, an awful churning emptiness in her gut. Whatever that feeling was, it prodded Lottie's cold reply.

"I don't see much different about you."

Patrice seemed undeterred by Lottie's efforts to be callous. Still standing on a step above her, Patrice placed her hands on Lottie's shoulders and pulled her closer. Her large brown eyes focused on Lottie's with an intensity that left the latter a bit weak in the knees. This further confused Lottie's anger with that something else she dared not name.

"Lottie, dismiss me if you wish, but I care what happens to you. I always have. If we survive the Yankees, I should like to be your friend."

"What you got there Patrice? Caught yourself some Bratcher trash?"

27

The voice was a familiar one to Lottie. It belonged to her half-brother, Calvin Edwards. A short, fat, red-faced runt who had tormented Lottie all her days, he was accompanied by a few more just like him. Calvin's followers laughed at his most recent pronouncement.

"Watch your mouth Calvin, it's going to cause you some pain," Patrice said.

"I don't need you to take up for me," Lottie said, as she pulled away from Patrice's touch.

"Oh, I wasn't taking up for you, Lottie," Patrice said while chuckling. "It was a warning. You're rocking on the cat's tail, Mr. Edwards. I'd watch my step."

"My father's bastard children are no concern of mine. Her ma's no more than a whore, and a poor one at that. You know, Lottie, he's got a much younger one now."

"The unfortunate circumstances of my birth seem to be on your mind every time I see you, Calvin. So it must concern you some. Your daddy is a bastard himself, and you know it as well as I do. So take your highfalutin airs back up those stairs, before I shoot a hole through you."

Patrice laughed under her breath, enjoying the moment.

"Patrice, your Pa's looking for ya'," Calvin said, as he glared at Lottie. His friends had already abandoned him, preventing him from displaying the same bravado on his exit that had accompanied his entrance.

"I must go, Lottie. Why don't you wait for us out front and my brother and I will ride part of the way home with you? You'll be safer that way."

"It will be a cold day in hell when I need a Cole to protect me."

And with that Lottie turned on her heel and left the way she came. She had all the information she needed, and she had to get away from Patrice.

"By the way Lottie, these shoes belong to a dead cousin, and this was to be her marriage suit. She took her own life when her beau came home in a pine box. Her mother said she hated to bury her in such good clothes when there was so much need."

Lottie slowed but did not stop. She just kept walking like the headstrong girl she was.

Patrice called after her, "You are going to be my friend, Lottie Bratcher. You just don't know it yet."

Chapter Four

Old Friends

When Lottie reached the spot where she left Big John, he was not there. She looked toward the street, checking for signs of cast-off would-be riders. All was clear, and Lottie almost let herself worry about him, but then she heard the familiar snort behind her. The massive animal nibbled softly on her shoulder as if to apologize for wandering off.

"Did you find some better grass, big man?"

Big John looked back over his shoulder at the line of horses tied outside the courthouse, with the black grooms left to watch over them.

"Oh, I see. You were struttin' for the girls. Let's get outta here before the Yankees come and those idiots in there try to deal with them. I will be glad when this whole thing is said and done."

She tapped Big John on the shoulder. He repeated their mounting ritual. Lottie was tall enough to use the stirrup, but it was simpler this way. At the moment she landed in the saddle, Lottie looked up at the courthouse. Patrice waved from a second-story window. Lottie pretended not to see her.

She settled in on Big John's back and mumbled to herself, "That girl makes me…I don't know what all."

Lottie clucked to Big John, and the two set off up Walnut, turning right on John Street to avoid the masses on the central thoroughfare. John Street became Stantonsburg Road on the edge of town where Lottie rejoined the main line of refugees steadily moving north.

A series of marshes, swamps, and sandy loom hills divided by rivers and streams made up the geography of Wayne County. There were few roads and fewer bridges for crossing the overflowing swamps. The rain had stopped, but the paths were far from dry. Thousands of wheels had created huge ruts, deep enough at some points to topple wagons, spilling the contents of whole lives along the pathway.

Lottie stayed off the main road to avoid the broken down wagons and the horde clogging the path. The evergreen canopy and pine needle-strewn forest floor kept the underbrush down, making it easy to parallel the Stantonsburg Road to Pate Town. She then turned east for about a quarter of a mile to a branch of The Slough and followed it northward. Lottie would have to cross The Slough and Nahunta Swamp to complete the trip home. As the fleeing horde made a mad dash for the few crossings that had not flooded out or been destroyed by the Confederates in their retreat, Lottie and Big John moved away from the road toward Jacob's Landing.

Jacob Saul, a formidable man in his day and now old and gray, still cast a hulking shadow in any doorway. He was born to a slave mother, the son of a wealthy planter. Jacob's father paid one thousand dollars at his birth, a bond to the state guaranteeing he would be a good Negro. This granted Jacob the status of a freeman of colour, subject to North Carolina law that stated any free "person of colour" was required to avoid "idleness and dissipation" in order to avoid arrest and a subsequent "term of time to service and labour."

Jacob and Lottie shared the heritage of being rich white men's bastard children. Granted, it was harder to be a proud black man than a proud poor white girl in the South's caste system. Jacob stayed in Wayne County near his mother, while she lived. The land he inherited allowed him to run a small raft across the Nahunta Swamp. The ferry system he developed was widely used. Jacob cut lumber off his property and floated it down the river to the mill for extra income. Whatever else he needed, Jacob said the Lord and the swamp would provide.

The ferryman had done quite well during the war, as he was known for his ability to move things around without being noticed.

He knew these swampy lands better than any man alive, black or white. Not all of what Jacob ferried could be called legal or even wise for a black man in the south, but neither was staying at home when he could have gone north.

Lottie loved Jacob. He, like her, was prideful and would never let his birth dictate his circumstances. He was a freeman, but he knew the slave life and spent many hours retelling tales he learned from his mother's ancestry. These were exciting stories to Lottie, who relished in the secret lives of the slave quarter. Of particular interest were the whisperings of the hidden places in the swamps where slaves gathered to dance and sing in ways banned by their owners, or to hide from the overseer's lash.

Lottie's mother introduced her to Jacob's Landing. She knew from the first visit on that two things would be happening whenever she arrived. Something good would be cooking, and Jacob would be singing. Jacob's pig in the ground barbecue was a dish sent from the gods. Lottie smelled the bacon fat long before she could see the cabin sitting on poles up in the treetops. She leaned her head back and took in the first rays of sunshine she had felt on her face in days. The warmth she desperately needed seeped into her chilled soul.

"Hello in the cabin," Lottie called.

Big John stepped around the corner of the path, revealing the cabin and a huge man looking down on them from the front deck.

"Hello, yourself. It looks like you done brung the sunshine wid ya."

Just then a shell exploded in the distance, northeast of Goldsborough. Closer now, it appeared the blue army had begun to surround its target destination.

"Dem Yankees don' be chasin you, is they?"

"Nope, not this time Jacob. You reckon me and Big John could get a ride on over to the other side. The road is jammed up with refugees tryin' to get to Raleigh or anywhere other than here."

"Settle Big John down below an' come on up. We'll have a little sumptin t'eat, do a little jawin', and den I see if I can get ya on your way."

Lottie placed Big John near some dry hay under the house and bounded up the stairs two at a time. When she reached the top, Jacob grabbed her in a bear hug.

"Good Lordy, Miss Lottie. You growin' to be a fine lady, fine lady, even if you don' know how to act like one," he chuckled. "Whatcha doin' out at a time like dis, wid them bluecoats a comin' so close."

"Had to go into town for the cure for Ma and the leg is no better, either."

Jacob's eyes seem to sparkle as he led Lottie into the cabin. A fire crackled in the stone hearth, where two large cast iron pots steamed with a heavenly odor. Nothing else could make one feel as warm inside as the smell of Jacob's wild-game stew unless it was eating it.

When Lottie had removed her wet oil coat and planter's hat she settled down at the table, feeling warm and safe for the first time all day. She marveled at the hearth, hand built from stones carried one by one from a local quarry. Jacob had told her the story of this land and this house many years ago. They were sitting in the same room surrounded by family, both hers and his.

All eyes had been focused on Jacob as he rocked back and forth in the big rocker by the fire. Lottie sat on her mother's lap, while the other children sat around ready to listen to a well-worn, yet well-loved story.

"When I was first given dis here piece of land by an old man tryin' to make up for his evil jus' before the Lord dun sent him to justice, nobody made nuttin out'in it cus it was a worthless piece of swamp, just good enough for a nigger. Even the black folks made fun of me."

All in the room laughed in anticipation of what was to come.

"What dem folks didn' know, was dat I's lived most of my life in dis swamp and could make a livin off'n it too. Owning land made me special. I could go and come as I pleased. I was recognized. I fished dis river and carried the fresh fish into the Griswold Hotel, and on the way back I would bring a rock from the quarry. I took special care to pick the best rock for each trip. I cut timber off the land and floated it down to the mill, polin' back against the current the supplies I traded for." He stopped just long enough to spit in the fire, his eyes far away on the river some years ago.

"We lived on the highest part of the land while the boys was young, but the freshets hit hard every spring. I come up with puttin' us a house on poles, up out of the water. Finding the big logs for the stilts under the house was the hardest part. I walked and floated dese swamps until one day, back in fifty-one it was, I found four black gum trees growin' in a diamond shape in the middle of a little sandbar. I wasn't really sure where I was. Somehow I got turned around. Nuthin looked familiar. I thought if I left to find out who owned the land I might never find dem trees again. I decided to cut 'em down and pay for 'em later. Surely no one had been dis far into the swamp and cared for the trees being cut down. I cut dose monsters down and tied 'em to my boat for the trip back. I tied 'em end to end to ease the burden and started polin'." Another hiss from the fire as he spat again and took in a deep breath.

"I tell you chil'ren, I have never been so dog-tired in all my days. I pushed dat little boat through the swamp in the direction of the sun. I knew if I went west I'd at least hit dry land before dark. But I didn't. I laid down in dat boat and prayed to Jesus he would see me through dat dark night. Everywhere in the dark were glowin' eyes an' strange sounds. Dat's when I heard the scariest sound in the world, the dogs was comin. Dey was trackin' through the swamp, splashing and howling as dey got closer."

One of the littlest children gasped, as the older kids smiled at the memory of their first time experiencing Jacob's plight.

"What was I gonna do? I's in the swamp at night with a load of lumber, dat won't 'sactly mine, yet. I couldn't move, I didn't know where I was, and the sounds seemed to come from everywhere. I laid low in dat boat, so low I swore my heart was causing ripples on the water every time it pounded. Den suddenly the splashin' grew very loud by the back of the boat and den the sound of a body tripping over one of dem floatin' logs. Splash!"

All the children leaned in a little closer.

"I was too scairt to look and too scairt not to look. I felt the cold hand of fear on my chest. I peeked over the end of the boat just in time to see a black figure rise up right over my head. I tried to scream, but a hand clamped down on my mouth. A voice of an angel said, 'You here on the railroad chil', don' make no sound."

This time when he spat, he dribbled a little on his chin. Stopping to wipe it off, he made his audience wait, which Lottie was sure was his intention.

Jacob's youngest son, John, even though he knew, still begged, "Papa, that angel, what she do?"

"The angel looked at me showin' only the whites of her eyes. She motioned for two men to follow her out of the bushes and join her near my boat. Now I was really shakin' cus the white man gonna fine me wid dese here runaways and lump me in amongst 'em. But the angel, she made me feel peaceful when she placed her hand on my arm. Slowly she turned to the men and dey lay down in the water side the boat and pushed us silently away from dem barking dogs."

"She seemed to know where she was heading so I lay down in the bottom of dat boat and presently I fell to sleep. When I come around next, it was mornin', and I was back near to the place we was stayin'. I thought maybe it had all been a dream, but later dat day as I was haulin dem logs up to shore, I seen hung on one of dem big trees a tear o' cloth. It was the same as dat angel been wearin' and I know'd it to be the truth. Dat's why dis house is blessed, cause an angel brung dese gum logs to me. An dey is the foundation of dis fam'ly home."

Jacob's booming voice brought Lottie back to the present. "Lord have mercy, girl, you done gone a day-dreamin' on me. You want some coffee? It's real coffee from Brazil. Folks tradin' all kinds of belongings to cross dat swamp dese days. A man would be a fool to take dat rebel script, so food is as good as gold 'round here."

"You are a wise man, Jacob. I would sure appreciate some good coffee. We've had only sweet potato grinds for a while now."

"Course, I done carried most of what's worth much away from here. But I saved the coffee, cause I knowed someone would come and be in need of it. And you looks to be that one. There's a lot on dat young mind. Sit, rest a spell." Jacob chuckled and hummed, as he went about pouring up the coffee.

Lottie gazed out of the broad front windows that opened onto a view of The Slough and the far shoreline. Building his house on stilts not only protected him from the spring floods but also afforded him a glimpse of prospective customers across the way. Lottie turned from the landscape and was drawn to several postcards and pictures on the mantle. Jacob had two sons, Jacob, Jr., and Rubin. He had sent them away from the south long before the war had begun. Jacob did so knowing that a freeman of colour gone from North Carolina more than ninety days could not return.

He had not seen his sons since the day they left on a steamer from Wilmington.

Jacob, Jr. was a sailor in New York and sent his father postcards from around the world. Jacob could not read, but he loved the pictures and had the cards read to him regularly by guests. Rubin was in school in Pennsylvania. A photo of the family, including Jacob's wife Mary, held the place of honor on the mantle. Mary died right before the war started. Jacob was in the habit of speaking to her as if she were still by his side.

As Jacob turned back from the fireplace with two steaming cups of coffee, he said casually to the vacant rocker, "Miss Mary, look who has come to see us. It's Thenia's girl, Lottie."

He paused and shook his head in agreement as if listening to someone speak.

"Yes'm, I agree she sure is a pretty girl."

Lottie smiled at the vacant chair in answer to Mary's comment, as any polite guest would. Suddenly conscious of wet hair sticking to her face, Lottie ran both hands through her curls which had grown much kinkier and tangled in this weather. Extracting a piece of leather from her pocket, she pulled her hair back into a bushy ponytail and tied it securely.

Lottie preferred her hair tied up or tucked away. It was unruly, dense, and a source of constant frustration. She would cut it all off if she were no longer forced to advertise her femininity in order to escape comment from the old women in town. It seemed to be everybody's business what Lottie Bratcher wore. She never understood why so many strongly objected to her "struttin' around" the streets of Goldsborough in men's trousers. No one rode a horse like Lottie did while wearing a dress, or trousers for that matter. What Lottie Bratcher did best of all was ride a horse, any horse, as fast as it could go. She didn't care to be wearing a skirt while doing it.

When last she'd reacted to Jane's constant nagging, Lottie told her, "This family can't waste money on fancy riding skirts to appease the town gossips, including you."

The cannonading boomed in rhythm now, like thunder coming on the wind.

"Jacob, the Yankees are coming right on into Goldsborough. Heard the mayor was to surrender the town when they get here.

They are already in Webbtown, and the last of the cavalry was said to be flyin' out of there, firin' over their shoulders."

"Dat close, huh?"

Lottie shrugged her shoulders. "You know how stories passed down the road can be. I don't think they'll come this way. I think they'll turn west. They aim to have Raleigh. Still, you might think about moving on for a bit."

"Don' you worry 'bout ol' Jacob. I been cookin' up all of what I have and loadin' it on dat raft yonder. I done carried off my tack and tools, hid 'em deep in the swamp. Don' want to leave nuthin' behind worth stealin'. Dem bummers be comin' out this far, even if the reg'lar army don't make it. An you best be watchin' for sum dem what's come home a'fore der time and is hidin' in dese parts. Most of dem are thieves anyhow and deserters. Don' you be fooled by no gray jacket, you mind my words."

His words stung a little. Deserters were as low as snakes for the most part. He saw what she was thinking.

"You know I ain't speakin' low 'bout our boys. They done der part in this here war. Don't let nobody tell you diff'rent."

The coffee went smoothly down without the bitter bite of burnt sweet potato she had grown accustomed to. It had been a quest of most country folk throughout the war to create a palatable coffee substitute, as what real coffee that came in went to the troops. So far Lottie was sure no one had even come close. Most of the time it tasted like hot water with burnt dirt in it, but this was real coffee. She closed her eyes and felt the warmth flow through her body.

When she opened her eyes again, Jacob had placed a bowl of stew in front of her with a plate of cornbread dripping butter from the sides. Lottie suddenly realized how hungry she was and dove into the food without even saying thank you. Her enthusiasm for the feast was all the appreciation Jacob needed. Cooking was his gift and spreading the joy his calling, Mary used to say.

Jacob asked about her family and she about his. Between gulps of food, they caught up with the health and welfare of all the loved ones. The conversation then turned to Jefferson.

"He's a might anxious with the Yankees so close. At least the patrols picking up deserters have dropped off now that the Rebs have retreated toward the Capital. Sherman will be in Raleigh in a few days, and then Lee is cut off for sure. I believe the end is near for the South. I only pray more of our boys make it home in one piece."

"Lord, ain't dat da truth. We done put too many in the ground already. An dis rain we been havin', the ol' folks say the Lord been tryin to wash the blood away."

Jacob rose and moved the big kettle off the fire.

"Looks like we'll have a full load for the crossin'," he said, glancing out the window.

Jacob must have sensed the approaching wagon before it came into view. Lottie stood and looked out the window, but saw nothing. Then just over the low hill, following the same path Lottie had taken, came a wagon overloaded with furniture and young children, being trailed by several older ones leading a sagging mule. These people had been traveling a long time, and it showed in their faces even from this distance. The blank stare of the refugees of Sherman's march was a recognizable feature that had become all too familiar in the last weeks.

It was unusual for anyone but locals to come down to Jacob's landing. It wasn't advertised on the main road due to the clandestine nature of Jacob's business associates during these war years. Secrecy had insured its success. Both the slaves and the white folks equally depended on Jacob's integrity, even if they didn't know it at the time. These new arrivals had obviously been many miles and seen horrible things, but they were not locals. Curiosity got the best of her. Lottie grabbed her coat and hat, and followed Jacob out the door.

Jacob walked a few steps ahead of her, carrying one of the heavy pots of stew down the steps toward a table by the water pump he had installed to draw water up from the river. The visitors disappeared from view as they wound their way down the path to the landing. The clanging of the pots tied on the back announced its position, as the wagon rattled through the washboard road created by the recent torrents.

Lottie checked on Big John who happily munched on hay. He never wore a bit with his bridle. Most men told her she needed one to control a horse that size. Lottie knew she didn't. If she needed Big John's attention, snatching his mouth bloody wasn't necessary. She simply asked. Unbuckling the saddle, Lottie pulled the heavy load from the horse's back. He looked over his shoulder, ears perked up in question.

"Nope, we aren't staying. I'm just going to dry your blanket out till we cross the Prong. Thought you might enjoy a little sun on your back."

She slapped the big horse's rump lovingly and led him from under the structure.

"Go, eat green things," Lottie told him. Big John needed lots of food to keep his huge frame healthy. She let him forage where he could. Just like the poor and displaced, animals suffered from lack of feed.

Lottie turned her attention from the horse just in time to see the wagon come into view. The man driving waved violently when he saw Jacob. A broad smile crossed his face.

"Jacob, you ol' man. How the hell are ya?"

The man pulled the wagon to a halt and climbed down hobbling on a cane toward Jacob, his arm out in anticipation of the bear hug to come.

Lottie wondered aloud, "Who the hell is that?"

Chapter Five

The Secret

Lottie had been guarding the secret for four months. A few select people knew the whereabouts of five young men absent without leave, but the task of keeping them safe rested with her. It was a burden she bore without complaint.

The populous essentially hated deserters, believing them cowards and scum. The most fanatical of those who wished deserters shot on sight, were the families who had lost sons, husbands, brothers, and fathers to the cause. Those folks needed to remember that the deserters were fathers, brothers, sons, husbands, and lovers too. Surely there were those who deserted out of pure cowardice, who deserved to be hated and despised. Yet, there were those men who had paid more than their fair share of dues in this long battle. With nothing left to give, they came home.

They came home to an impoverished South, to a Wayne County stripped of its beauty and bounty of old. Gone were the days of worrying only if there'd be enough rain, or if there would be too much. There were no more lazy evenings seated on the porch, listening to the sound of children sleeping and crickets singing. These men were not slave owners. If they owned land, it wasn't much. They were farm laborers from small little farms who raised crops and children, just everyday folk with no stake in the slave trade. They never had much, never needed much, but now they had nothing.

If a deserter were lucky, he lived among sympathizers who knew what he had given up to the South and would shelter him from the army patrols that sought to imprison deserters or force them back to war. Some of the civilian patrols were worse. Filled with angry men who were too afraid to fight the Yankees, they were, however, inclined to shoot an unarmed deserter as their service to the cause. Jack Cole was just such a man.

So the five men, who deserted from Company C, 45th Regiment, North Carolina Infantry, on November 11, 1864, in Newtown, Va., were secreted away in Appletree Swamp. Lottie brought supplies and checked on the men as often as she safely could. Her brother James traveled unmolested to town and back home, with small stores he dropped off at Jacobs's over the last few weeks, in preparation for this day. Lottie eyed the stack of hay in the corner, knowing what it concealed and what she might have to do to protect it.

Turning toward the sound of Jacob's roaring laughter, Lottie saw him lift the man with the cane off the ground in a bear hug. This behavior was reserved for special people. She had to know who the limping man was, and above all, could he be trusted?

Lottie left the shelter and headed toward the men. She glanced at the wagon and the disembarking passengers. This man and woman could not be the parents of all these young ones. There were two toddlers and a goat that needed milking being helped down from the back of the wagon by two girls around ten. Two young boys followed the tall teenage boy leading the mule. The woman had a babe in her arms. As Lottie grew closer, she realized the woman could not be more than sixteen.

"Lottie, come on over here. One of the boys don' come home to roost. Y'all 'member Charlie Hunt, to be sure."

Lottie stood still. She peered out through the now bright sunlight. Looking hard, she saw it. That one dimple that made his grin irresistible and the way he cocked his head when he looked at her. She broke into a run.

"Charlie! Charlie! Oh, Charlie!"

She wrapped Charlie up in her arms. Tears began to flow from both of them. They spoke at the same time, two old friends reunited.

"Jeff will be so glad to see you. He wrote me that our own artillery at Gettysburg had hit your unit. He thinks you are dead."

"Well, here I am, such as I am; a broken down old man with a travelin' band of children that ain't even mine. This here is Rose. She's my sister Emma's daughter and sister to that babe there. I went to stay with Emma down in Georgia after the hospital turned me out. We lost her in childbirth. A nephew and the babe's father passed on along the way. Y'all little 'uns come over here."

The cluster of children waddled and strode, appropriate to age, over to the adults now gathered near the big stone table. The little girls placed the toddlers up on the table, while the others huddled close. The clothes the toddlers and girls wore were at one time very nice, but now the lace was stained with dirt and what appeared to be soot. The toddler's faces had been wiped clean, leaving grime-streaked, full moon shaped visages. If it were not so tragic, it would have been precious. Only the older girls had shoes.

The boys were a stark contrast to the female passengers. They were dirt covered from head to toe, with not one clean spot on any of them. The whites of their eyes were eerily bright in great disparity to their dirt-stained skin. The differing shades of mud and dirt were remarkable. The colors told the tale of the trail behind them, from the red clay of Georgia to the green marl colored mud of the bottoms and dark black of the swamps. The clothes were mere rags draped over the boys' bones.

"The four girls there are sisters. We found them in a burned out barn with the bodies of their parents. They've been with us since Columbia. The two little 'uns are Mary Elizabeth and Elizabeth Mary, twins."

Lottie looked at Rose and Charlie, and they all shared a laugh at the names and the way the twins were behaving as they realized the conversation was about them. Lottie could tell these had been pampered little babies, the apples of someone's eye.

"My name is Alice," the oldest of the two other girls said. She curtsied like a little princess. "And this is my sister Kate."

The smaller girl stepped forward, curtsied, and then immediately stepped back behind her sister. She stared at Jacob as if she had never seen anything so huge in all her life.

"You'll have to forgive them, Jacob. It was slaves led by some white men from up north that burned their place and killed their parents."

"Dat's all right, lots a little 'uns scared o' me, black and white. I bein' so big an' all. Candy usually take ker a dat and I got a plenty of it."

The older children lit up with smiles for the first time since Lottie first saw them.

"That tall boy there is Joseph and his brothers, Daniel, the middle one, and David, the smallest. They have been with us since Georgia. Said there was nothin' left to stay for, and they reckoned they'd like to see North Carolina, so they followed along."

"Why don' you chil'in' come wid me and have a bite to eat an some of dat candy I talked about."

Hunger doesn't know color and the children followed Jacob like the pied piper right on up the stairs and into the cabin. Joseph stopped at the foot of the stairs, where he lifted one of the Elizabeths into his arms. Daniel grabbed the other, and they ascended the stairs to what Lottie knew would be a meal they would never forget.

"Charlie, I'm going to take the baby up. He's so poorly, maybe Jacob will know what to do. I'll send one of the boys down to milk the goat."

"I'll be right up myself, Rose. I need to speak to Lottie a spell."

Rose was well out of earshot when Charlie took Lottie's hand and led her toward the water. In the distance, cannons boomed.

"Jefferson is good, you say? Where is his company now? Have you heard from him lately?"

"Charlie, did you know I was secretly in love with you when I was ten?"

Lottie had known Charles Harlan Hunt all her life. Until he was eighteen, he was her older brother's constant companion. He had gone to Georgia with family. Charlie had kept in touch with Jeff through letters. In a twist of fate, they wound up in the same division in the war, until Gettysburg.

Charlie was a rugged, good-looking, redhead. His curly hair poked out from under the rim of his hat. His sunny disposition made him a favorite of everyone he met. It was no wonder these folks had taken up with him on his journey. Charlie made people feel good.

"Had I known what a great beauty that scrawny kid would grow into, I would have stopped time and waited for you. Now, I'm an old man at twenty-five, and half a man at that." He lifted his cane, as if in explanation.

While he spoke, Lottie's mind raced. Charlie could be trusted. She had to believe that, or everything else in her life was worthless. She decided it was what Jeff would want.

"Lottie Bratcher, I have known you since the day you were born, and I know when you are hiding something. What is that mind of yours turning over? And what does it have to do with Jefferson?"

She had held the secret in for so long when she started speaking the words flew from her mouth in one long breath.

"Jeff and four of the men from his company are hiding in Appletree Swamp. He deserted back in November. Please, Charlie, don't judge him. Wait until you hear what he has to say."

"Lottie, Jeff is more of a brother to me than my own flesh and blood. If he left the army, he had a good reason."

"There are only two of us that know where they are, me and Jacob. A few more know they are here, but we thought we should keep the hiding place a secret."

"It's best you keep it that way. I'm gonna take these youngsters over to my uncle's place in Saratoga. Then I'll come to Bratcher Patch, and we'll go find the ol' boy and see what he has to say. Is he hurt?"

"No, but one of the other ones is. Harper has a bad leg wound. Dr. Davis gave me a cure to put on it, and we got a load of supplies under the shed for them. Jacob and I were just before heading that way."

"Old Doc is still around," Charlie laughed and shook his head. "Still witch doctorin' with Mary I suppose."

Lottie nodded and laughed along with Charlie. Suddenly, he put an arm around her shoulder and looked deep into her eyes. He could tell she had needed someone to share this burden with.

"Right smart timin' on my part, to get here when I did. Let me get a mouthful t'eat, and we'll be on our way."

The two old friends walked arm in arm toward the cabin. For the first time in four months, Lottie began to relax. It was nice to have someone to share the burden of this secret. Charlie coming now was like a miracle, and she was surely due one.

Chapter Six

The Float Trip

The little children resembled ticks about to pop when the starving travelers had finished eating everything Jacob had provided. The toddlers waned in and out of dreamland, little fingers stuck to remnants of hard candy, while they rested with Rose and the baby up on the porch. The rest of the group, slowed by full bellies, set about loading up for the trip. The cannonading from the southwest reminded everyone that time was of the essence.

Lottie, along with Joseph and his little brothers, loaded the supplies from under the shelter into the johnboat. Using a long pole, this small flat bottom boat could be navigated easily through the overflowing marsh and swamp. The recent rains were a godsend to Jacob. He would not need to leave the water to reach the boys. People seeing him on the swamp would see nothing unusual, just big ol' Jacob singing hymns and poling along.

Lottie had already moved Big John down to the water, where he enjoyed the sun on his back and the children, who at first were awed by his size, now took turns giving him little bits of peppermint candy they received from Jacob.

"Don't let him take all your candy. He is a hound for sweets. Big John, you be nice now, and say thank you."

Big John shook his head up and down and whinnied, which delighted the children even more. This produced the desired results as far as Big John was concerned. The children, once over the laughing fit the first thank you induced, quickly dug around in their pockets for more candy. Lottie was enjoying the young ones' fun when Jacob and Charlie arrived at the landing with the overloaded wagon.

The two Elizabeth's drowsily took their places on the makeshift bed in the back of the wagon and were asleep as soon as their curly heads hit the pillow. Rose, still cradling the baby, seated herself beside Charlie, who at the moment was having a little trouble convincing his mules that the barge he was attempting to load them on would actually hold. Jacob stepped in front of them and pretty as you please the mules followed him on. Jacob's way with children extended to animals.

The barge was large enough for two wagons and was pulled across The Slough by a series of ropes and pulleys Jacob had set up over the years. He could winch a barge through much of northeastern Wayne and part of Green County. Musgrave Crossroads, the destination of the passengers today, lay to the north. With everything loaded and the johnboat tied to the barge, the party set off.

Jacob had closed up the cabin, but not before removing his pictures and postcards. The Yankees would have to be looking for the landing to find it, but Jacob wasn't taking any chances trusting the folks that did know where he lived. Going through the cabin one last time, he removed his most treasured possessions and added them to the bundles in the johnboat tied to the back of the barge. Mary's rocking chair was the last thing to leave the cabin.

"Come along, Miss Mary," Jacob said, as he lowered the rocker into the boat. "We goin' on a float trip."

Once the loads and people were secure, Jacob began turning the winch that caused the rope line to snap up out of the water, where it stayed out of the way of other boats until in use. It was astounding how Jacob had set up the pulley system with its switching stations for differing directions. The swamps and channels spread out all over Wayne and Greene counties. Jacob could travel almost anywhere with his system.

This particular trip had the barge traveling up the north leg of The Slough, making an easterly turn following the main branch into Nahunta Swamp. Nahunta Swamp spread over much of northeastern Wayne County, flowing into Contentnea Creek in

47

Greene County. The many feeder streams along the Nahunta's traverses allowed access to most of the area by flatboat.

The older children settled in for long overdue naps after the initial wonder of the trip wore off. Still cradling the now contented babe, Rose nodded off to the gentle rocking of the barge as it glided through the water. The weather had turned off pretty, and the water's smooth surface looked thick and slow when moved by the small waves the barge created. Jacob turned the winch in a steady rhythm and began to sing one of his favorite spirituals. His deep bass rumbled across the water, soft and low.

"The Gospel train's comin', don'tcha wanna go? The Gospel train's comin', don'tcha wanna go? The Gospel train's comin', don'tcha wanna go? Oh, Lawd, yes, I wanna go. She's comin' 'round the mountain, don'tcha wanna go…"

Lottie and Charlie leaned against the side rail catching up on the last seven years.

"After you left, Jefferson moved over to Bullhead. He worked there as a hand until just before the war. Then he went over to Guilford County to work with Allen Bratcher on Uncle Matthew's place. When the call went out to sign up, Allen went the first day, and Jeff followed right behind him."

"That's pretty much what happened in Georgia. I was farmin' one day and fightin' the next. Pure damn luck, my regiment gettin' lumped in with Jefferson's in Rode's Corps. We had us a time, Lott. Chasin' bluecoats."

Charlie chuckled, but a pall fell over his face and his smile faded. He appeared to try to swallow his emotions, before he continued, "We were going to be home by Christmas. They told us that's why we were fighting, that is what we were protecting— hearth and home."

He stopped to look at Lottie. "You know, Lott. I don't think a Yankee would have ever stepped foot on that farm we got burned out of in Georgia if those rich fellas hadn't started this war."

His eyes grew glazed with the same faraway stare Jefferson so often wore. She knew it was time to change the subject.

"I've been farmin' Gran-mammy's land and helpin' James out on the parcel his pa gave 'em. James got shot in the first battle of Goldsborough, lost a leg."

"Still don't care for Hub Edwards, I see. He's your pa too. You wouldn't 'a had Big John there if he hadn't give 'im to ya'."

"Lotta water under that bridge, Charlie. Big John is the only thing that man ever gave me. As much as I love this animal, he's a small payment on the debt Hub Edwards owes!"

"He took care of your family when he still could. That's more than most."

"Money isn't everything. Might as well be walking around with a letter on my chest. A child ought not to have to hear folks saying, 'There's that whore Bratcher woman and all those Edwards' bastards.' "

"Them old biddies talk about each other when out of earshot. Don't pay no mind to what folks think of ya, Lott. It's what you make of yourself that counts. Bastards have been kings and queens. And Lottie, you're selling your ma short. Everybody around here that knows Parthenia understands what happened. Your pa done right by your ma. You'll see it someday."

Unmoved by Charlie's prediction, Lottie launched into a tirade about her father.

"His breed of men is the cause of this infernal war. Egotistical patriarchs with money and power who feel the need to spread their seed among the less fortunate, creating minute kingdoms to rule. Trips to the slave quarter bring mulatto children. Nightly visits to the white servants' rooms produce whole families of bastards to worship at the great man's feet." Lottie was near seething now. "I won't be forced into that life. I won't be a part of that world."

"This is more than your pa we're talking about. What's got you so outta sorts?"

Charlie apparently noted the set of Lottie's jaw. He patted her shoulder and wandered forward to where Jacob was tending the line. Lottie looked up at Big John, who at the moment was making moon-eyes at Charlie's mule. Lottie's own eyelids fluttered shut while she listened to the soft slap, slap of the ripples against the barge, as it floated downstream toward Nahunta. Soon she was drifting back to the first time she ever saw the little black colt with the star on his forehead.

Nine years old and already tall for her age, Lottie stood on the lowest rail of the corral fence and hung her elbows over the top one. She watched the new load of horses from Georgia arrive. Hub

Edwards thought himself a horseman and invested heavily in the thoroughbreds his father found for him in Georgia.

Hub Edwards was himself the bastard child of a wealthy landowner. Brantley Edwards had lived with Hub's mother on the land Hub now called his own. Brantley was young and rebellious when he started his family with his mistress, at the vigorous objection of his father.

"You support your whore, Brantley. Build 'er a house, buy her pretty things, but you don't live with them," old man Edwards had said, according to the tales Lottie heard from family gossip.

Once he realized his days would be more labor than love, his dreams of the life of a gentleman farmer imploded, Brantley gave in to his father's wishes. He left his lover and young son behind, going to Georgia to settle land the Edwards family claimed through Revolutionary War pensions. Once there he remarried and lived out the rest of his days with his legitimate family. Brantley's father had seen to it that his son would marry a dowry to enlarge the family fortunes and robbed Hub of his ancestry.

Brantley did give Hub his surname, claimed him on a court bond, and gifted him his lands in North Carolina. A name and some dirt changed Hubbard from just another poorhouse bastard into a member of the landed gentry. After all, southern aristocracy finds its roots in the feudal system, where first sons were often bastards who fought the legitimate heir for the throne.

It was this fact that puzzled Lottie, as she grew old enough to understand that society treated people differently according to class. How could a man, whose father was taken away from him because of the social standing of his mother, turn around and populate the world with bastards of his own? He granted land to Parthenia, James, and Jefferson. Payment for his sins and the sons he made, in Lottie's way of thinking. It puzzled her how the illegitimacy of a male child could be cleansed by a land deed.

What about his daughters? Hub doomed them to relive their mother's and mother's mother's lives before them—that of a mistress or some poor farmer's last chance. He saw to it that they were fed, clothed, and securely housed. He made sure they received some schooling. Lottie was given access to Hub's library, where she read about the world and ultimately learned who she was. The day she read The Scarlet Letter, Lottie left her father's house, never to return. She knew nothing would ever remove the permanent scar of illegitimacy. Charlotte Bratcher's name would always be in the county bastardy bond book for all of history to see.

But, these thoughts were far from the nine-year-old Lottie's mind. That day long ago, her cares were only for horses, the single passion of her young life.

"Are they here yet?"

The voice of Hub Edwards drew young Lottie's attention away from the barn. She hopped down from the fence and skipped towards her father. Hubbard Brantley Edwards was tall and handsome. He had the bone structure of the landed gentry, delicate features with long elegant limbs. The curls on his head were soft brown with golden highlights, as were his daughter's. His neatly trimmed beard and mustache glittered, the blonde hairs reflecting the sun like gold dust. He wore a burgundy vest with a grey frock coat that day. Lottie was proud to be the daughter of this attractive smiling man. He reached for her hand and walked with her to the barn. Lottie and Hub looked like any father and daughter, hand in hand on a sunny spring day.

"Pa, do you think she'll be as fast as Lexington?"

Her father had read her stories of the famous horse, the fastest four-mile thoroughbred in the United States, time seven minutes nineteen and three quarter seconds.

"We'll have to run her and see, but first we have to let her get her legs back."

"Did riding on the ship make her legs wobbly?"

"True it is a long trip from Georgia, by sea and land, but she had some other things to tend to on the trip."

"Pa, horses don't tend to nothin' but grain and manure." Lottie laughed at her own wittiness.

"That shows what you know, little missy. Look yonder."

The two entered the barn where Lottie froze. A spindly-legged black colt nursed at the teat of a beautiful black thoroughbred. Lottie began to move very slowly toward mother and son.

"Pa, she had a baby," her voice not more than a whisper.

At the sound of Lottie's voice, the little black colt turned his head away from his mother and looked Lottie in the eyes. The foal had a broad forehead stamped with a four-point white star, which appeared to have been painted on. The tail of the blaze trailed down his nose. His wide-set eyes were bright and curious. He nodded at Lottie and went back to his meal.

"What do you think, Lott? Should we keep him?"

"Oh yes! He's the most beautiful colt I've ever seen."

"Look how big he is already. He may be too big to race."

"He's perfect, Pa. You have to keep him."

"Of all my children, you share my enthusiasm for horses. I shall trust your good eye and make the bill of sale official, only I need to know what to call him."

"Pa, you always name the horses."

"Yes, because they are mine. However, the bill of sale in question says he belongs to you. Now, what shall we name him?"

Lottie could hear nothing but her heart pounding in her ears. She looked up at her father beaming down at her, enjoying the moment as much as she. Finally able to move again she threw her arms around Hub Edwards.

"Thank you, Pa. I'll never want another thing. He is all I have ever wanted."

"Hold her to that Hub," a woman's voice laughed behind them.

"Parthenia, your daughter and I were just discussing the name of her new charge there."

"Ma, just look at him. He's perfect."

Lottie left the adults and went over to observe the colt more closely.

"Hub, I appreciate what you have done, but you know Harriet is going to pitch a fit."

"And what would be unusual about that. My wife is in a constant state of fit pitching."

"She takes it out on the children. I can't watch them all the time. She's hateful."

The barn door creaked open a few more feet. Standing in the glare of the sun was the unmistakably round silhouette of Harriet Lane Edwards.

"You were saying," drawled Harriet.

"She was saying what an insufferable hag you can be, and I agreed with her."

"What pleasant talk for such a lovely afternoon. What have we here? New bloodlines for the farm? What a lovely colt. He will make a fine saddle horse for Calvin."

Lottie was stricken with fear. She hated Harriet and for a good reason. Her father's wife made it her mission in life to assure that all bastards on the farm knew their place. She begrudged every kindness shown to children other than her own.

"The colt belongs to Lottie. I reckon she'll decide who'll be ridin' him."

"Hubbard Edwards, if you wish to waste your money it is your business. I merely came down to the barn to ask that you have the decency to have your whore keep her children away this afternoon. I am having the ladies over for tea and bible reading."

Harriet turned to leave.

"For such a God-fearin' woman, Harriet, you sure do spit the venom like the devil's own," Hub called after her.

No one spoke for a moment.

"Big John. I'm gonna call him Big John."

Parthenia questioned her daughter, "Why on earth are you going to call that animal Big John?"

"Well, he's going to be big, and me and Martha Ann are reading about Apostle John in bible study. It came to me that was his name."

Hubbard Edwards' laughter was still echoing in Lottie's mind when she realized she was being shaken awake. Charlie stood over her.

"Come on sleepy head. It's time to go to work."

The water was high and moving quickly out in the main channel of the swamp. Jacob decided that using the rudder and the poles would be faster than using the lines. Taking advantage of the speed of the freshet and the natural flow of the swamp, the trip would take less time. With all hands joined in, soon the barge filled with laughter and Jacob's voice singing. The breeze occasionally brought the soft thud of the cannon fire. Distance from the Yankees made the sailing party stronger, as fear loosened its tight grip momentarily.

When he reached Fayetteville, with its Confederate armory and stores, Sherman gave orders to destroy all property, public and private, which may give aid and comfort to the enemy. Sherman's troops, along with those of Generals Schofield and Terry, had taken this order to heart. A wide corridor had been cut through the coastal Carolina plains leaving a desolate and desperate people in its wake.

Lottie and her fellow passengers could see the gray smoke of burning cotton bales mixed with the distinctive yellow hue of artillery fire billowing upward over the trees on the southern horizon. Goldsborough was under siege. By now the Mayor's plan to surrender would have been put into action. They would know soon enough if the town were to be burned. Lottie searched the sky and did not see the ominous black smoke that would tell the tale.

The barge moved along swiftly, approaching the turn to the grove and then north along Nahunta Swamp. They would now move upstream and would once again be forced to use the winch line. The barge began to slow as Jacob turned toward the shoreline and his switching station. His skillful hand guided the fat-bodied barge into place, where he quickly hooked the line into the winch. The barge and its passengers soon headed northwest. Once more Lottie glanced back for signs of Goldsborough's fiery end and saw none, before the dense swamp canopy swallowed the sky.

Southern long moss covered bald-cypress trees rising up out of the murky water in every direction. The sun filtered through the canopy above, creating an eerie green glow that engulfed the very air. The occupants of the ferry hushed without being asked. Occasionally a cypress knee would cause a start, appearing as a swamp fiend spying from the murk. Frogs and bugs called to each other, singing lustily of the coming of spring.

From above, Lottie heard, "Creeeaaaakkkkk," as the breeze swayed the trees slightly causing the thick limbs of the ancient trees to rub against one another. The winch clicked along. Only the occasional bumping of the poles, manned by Charlie and Lottie, interrupted the steady, "Click, click, click."

After traveling a little over a mile up the eastern branch of Nahunta Swamp, the band reached their destination. Charlie and his lot would be going west, on to Musgrave Crossroads, and then take a northerly turn joining back up with the Stantonsburg Road. Lottie would head northeast toward Faro and beyond to Bratcher Patch on the South Fork of Appletree Swamp. These roads were not much more than farm to market wagon paths, but would be less traveled than the main accesses.

Once Charlie's group had been carefully deposited on the western shore, he and Lottie walked away from the others.

"Tell Jefferson his brother has come home. I will join you at your place in a day or two. I've got to get these young ones settled into homes first, but I'll be back soon."

Lottie nodded understanding and asked, "Do you have a pistol? You still have a bit of traveling to do. The refugees are getting desperate, and folks are scared."

"Pistol and shot at the ready. I did not live through Gettysburg to die in sight of home."

"Then until we meet again." Lottie hugged Charlie tightly. Through tears of happiness, she whispered, "I'm so happy you are home, Charlie."

Charlie stood her in front of him, hands clasping her shoulders. "You be safe. I'll be back before you know it."

Lottie hopped back on the barge for the trip to the eastern shore. She looked back only once to wave goodbye while chastising herself for becoming so emotional. She saddled Big John, preparing for the next leg of the trip. This part of the journey Big John could do without being led. If Lottie let him run, they would be home in an hour. She reached into her saddlebag and extracted the package she had received from Mary.

"Jacob, I'm going to take Ma's cure out of this bundle and give you the rest to take to Jefferson. Mary left Doc's notes in with the herbs, so Jeff will know what to do with them."

"I'll be leavin' the barge here and takin' the flatboat the rest 'a the way. Should catch up to the boys early evenin'."

The two conspirators talked in hushed tones as they tied up the barge.

"Tell them what happened in Goldsborough today, and tell Jeff that I'll be coming soon as I can. I'll bring Charlie, but let it be a surprise."

"I'll relate the news of the day as I know it, now you best be gittin' on."

Lottie climbed aboard Big John. He was ready to stretch his legs and pranced about.

Lottie smiled at Jacob, "You're a good man Jacob Saul. God bless you."

Lottie clucked to Big John and turned down the well-used path heading for home.

Chapter Seven

Evil Eyes

The woods surrounding the path were alive with the mating calls of toads and insects. The natural world relished the abundant rains awakening the swamp from the slumber of winter. Lottie leaned into Big John's neck and let him run at his leisure. The chorus trumpeting spring's arrival became lost in the sound of his thundering hoofs echoing through the dense forest.

Old Indian trails cut through the thick woodlands in the northeast corner of Wayne County. The Tuscarora tribe called this part of the Carolina colonies home for many years before the white man decided they had to go. The raids by natives on poor defenseless pioneers were the fodder of fireside stories for generations, even if they lacked a basis in fact. There wasn't a child around who hadn't been told to stay out of the swamp because some of King Tom's warriors still hid in the cypress knees and their favorite meal happened to be small children.

They were coming up on a clearing when Big John suddenly slowed and flared his nostrils. Lottie brought the big horse to a stop and listened.

"Good boy," she whispered.

Lottie stood up in the stirrups, craned her neck, and stared into the glare of sunlight at the edge of the clearing. She cautiously led Big John to the side of the path and waited. The horse under her felt the tension in her thighs and quieted like any prey animal would when a predator is near.

They were not invisible, but would at least have the advantage of seeing anyone approaching before they saw her. Big John's ears scoped the woods to her left. Then she heard it. Horses crunched through the bramble. They were not in a hurry, picking the way slowly, making almost no sound, not more than a hundred feet away.

Lottie backed Big John into the shadows. She peered through the thick forest, searching for the approaching horses. The riders' course seemed to be taking them across the path and deeper into Nahunta Swamp. If it was the home guard, Lottie could expect nothing more than hazing. She had grown up with most of them and parties on both sides knew well enough not to push things too far. Deserters rarely had horses. If it were Yankees or thieves, Lottie would just as soon they go on their way without knowing she was there. Nonetheless, she took hold of her pistol and crouched lower in the saddle.

The encroaching force came to a stop just off the path. Then cautiously the men appeared out of the trees just inside Lottie's field of view. Through the branches she counted five men on horseback, each leading an unsaddled horse behind his own mount. A man in a black planter's hat seemed to be in charge. He led no stock and motioned the others when to cross.

The man in the black hat sent chills down Lottie's spine. She had never seen this man before, but she could feel his presence. He was an evil man to be sure. He had a leathered face with a salt and pepper mustache twirled at the ends into a greasy pinwheel of considerable length. He wasn't large and sat slouched in the saddle. His mount was a real beauty, a bay with large brown frightened eyes. This was a cruel man. He was heavily armed, as were his men. Lottie watched the man scan the very spot where she hid. He had cold eyes that peered out through tightly pinched wrinkles so deep they never slackened. She held her breath and could avow Big John did too.

When the sun begins to bake a well-dampened flat land, a low fog commences and hangs in the air all day and night. At that very moment, the fog rolled into the forest and enveloped Lottie in a welcomed haze. She knew she could not be seen, because she could not, at the moment, see anything but her mount's ears still at attention. She waited there, barely breathing until she felt Big John relax under her. She trusted him with her life and once again he had saved her.

"Good boy," she whispered and nudged him back onto the path.

She moved slowly toward the clearing and only took a deep breath when she saw Faro rise up in front of her. Faro village was astir with the news of Yankees. It struck Lottie how the haze hung in the middle of the buildings, revealing only the tops and bottoms of the structures. This was not home, but close enough to run to safety. Lottie tucked away her weapon and let Big John stretch out to run as hard as he pleased. They passed below the village and entered the south branch of Appletree Swamp, where Bratcher Patch lay just ahead. One more clump of trees and Lottie could relax.

Big John worked up a lather, as they approached the fork in the road. If Lottie took the left fork into Faro, she would wind her way to Eureka and then on to Black Creek or Stantonsburg. Choosing the right fork, she proceeded straight for the middle of Appletree Swamp and the land purchased by Lottie's grandfather Phillip from old man Edwards. The farm next door belonged to Lottie's father, but through the grace of God, as far as Lottie was concerned, he had moved before the war back to Bullhead in Green County, to a family plantation.

Bullhead had gotten its name during the Revolutionary War. A wealthy planter's property was about to be invaded by Cornwallis' troops. The family set loose a large, angry bull to dissuade the soldiers from entering the yard. The red in the British uniforms drove the bull wild, but the effect was short-lived. The troops killed the bull, cooked him, and hung its head up in a large tree in the yard. The area has been called Bullhead from that day forward.

Lottie squeezed her knees into Big John's sides, asking him for all he had. He could smell home too and gave her a thrilling run. She could see very little through the mist and pushed through on instinct. As they burst out of the trees and into the clearing, home appeared. The haze lifted enough to show the smoke coming from the chimneys. The smell of pork fat reached her nose. Good, supper was ready.

An elm standing nearly one hundred feet tall with a trunk measured at four feet in diameter towered over the weathered farmhouse centered in Bratcher Patch. No grass had grown in the yard for years. The ground was swept clean with yard brooms, rudimentary fire protection for the structures that housed and fed the family. The earth felt like fine powder under bare feet, pounded smooth by four generations of Bratchers.

In front of the main house, a vast cultivated field awaited the warmth of spring. The family garden occupied a low rolling hill on the left side of the property. The grade made for excellent drainage and had served that purpose well in the recent deluge. The outhouse, stable, and corral had been built on the next rise, on the other side of the garden, away from and usually downwind of the house. A corncrib, chicken coop, and smokehouse set off from the back of the house, just before the yard sloped off toward the low ground.

Below the house, the grass started to grow again on an embankment that led to a small stream. Near the water and a safe distance from the house, stood two tobacco barns built upon brick piers. A fire was a constant worry with smoke-cured tobacco. James and Jane had their own homes on the other side of the barns, about fifty yards away. Behind the tobacco barns, on the edge of the woods, the family had a small lumber mill and tool shed.

A broad veranda wrapped around the house, with a sleeping porch on the south side. The kitchen stood off from the main living quarters beside a small cabin. Lottie and James had built a sheltered walkway joining the back porch to the two structures. Her mother swore they had only created a wick to the main house, which they would be responsible for burning to the ground.

"There is a reason they didn't build the kitchen in the house," she protested.

The house used to be painted a bright white, but since the war paint was in short supply. They really should whitewash it this spring. The red tin roof was in want of repair. Lottie looked at her home, and all that needed done and tried to remember what her grandmother had said.

"If there weren't always somethin' to do, we wouldn't be necessary. I ain't ready to be under the ground, so I make sure I got somethin' to do above it every day."

At this rate, Lottie thought she would never die because there was always something to do at Bratcher Patch.

Her thirteen-year-old sister Sarah waited in the yard as Lottie drew up and dismounted.

"Lord, Lott, did you try to run him to death. He's all a lather."

"You loved it. Didn't you, big boy?" The big horse snorted and pawed the ground.

"I'll cool him down for you and brush him good."

"Get one of Aunt Lizzie's boys to help you with the saddle and packs."

"I can handle it, Lottie. I am nearly grown."

Lottie looked at her red-headed sister and smiled, "Well, I guess you are. Use the step stool. I did until I grew some."

Lottie grabbed the medicine from the pack and shoved it into her coat pocket. She patted Big John on the rump as Sarah led him away. Turning to look out in the field for James or one of his sons, she saw that no one was there. They must have already come in for the day. Dusk was closing in quickly.

Out of the twilight, Lottie caught sight of riders coming out of the woods near the path. Her heart started pounding, as she realized that these were the riders she had seen earlier. She recognized the black hat and the bay ridden by the first man.

Lottie glanced around the yard. At any other time there would be children, animals, men, and women so thick you have to watch your step, but at this moment Lottie stood alone. The old coonhound, near deaf and hopelessly blind, slept peacefully under the porch. Her pistol was tucked under the belt at her waist, in the small of her back, but Lottie dare not give that away by pulling one weapon against the many coming straight at her.

Next door, James would be preparing to bring the boys over for supper. Lizzie would be feeding everybody at the dining room table, including her own, cursing the mud as the clan filtered in. John Simpson, Jane's husband, could be seen a good hundred yards away on his porch staring at God knows what.

"A deaf and blind dog and a sorry excuse for a man to help me. I might as well just fall down and beg for mercy."

The riders were closer now, and Lottie could see the wrinkled eyes following the path Sarah had taken with Big John. The fine hairs stood on the back of Lottie's neck. Should she fire up in the

61

air to warn the approaching horsemen and her family inside? They might mistake a warning for an attack and kill her where she stood. Several of the riders carried rifles in the crooks of their arms.

Lottie made the first move without thinking; she just did it as it came to her. Removing her hat and untying her hair she shook it loose, the ringlets falling gracefully over her shoulders. She smiled at the approaching riders and saw them visibly relax as she came into view. Even trail dirt and a man's clothes could not disguise her femininity.

"Howdy. Are y'all lost?"

"No ma'am, we just seen the damnedest horse tear ass through that path back yonder and was wanting to get a good look at 'im. My name's Tiller, and these here are my hands."

"Tiller, you say. Don't know any Tillers from 'round here. You say these are your hands. What do they do for you?"

"We're rounding up horses for the army, and these boys work for me on my place in Virginia."

"Well, we don't have any horses to sell to the army. What we have we need to live and make more food that someone will confiscate to feed the damn army."

"The horse we saw weren't no working horse. And I never said we was buying horses for the army. We are taking horses for the army, and I'll be taking that one."

A devilish grin came over Tiller's face. He pulled his pistol and aimed it at Lottie.

"No woman who can ride a horse like that is to be trusted. Go get that horse, boys, and bring me that little girl. Now, you got any menfolk on this place?"

Two of the riders rode toward the stable. Lottie flinched for a moment and started to reach for the pistol, but thought better of it.

"The only menfolk we got are boys, and that beat up old soldier down there on that porch. John Simpson hasn't said a word or done anything, but sit right there for two years since the army sent him home. We think the war touched him in the head because there isn't a mark on him."

Lottie said all this through clenched teeth as she began to hear Sarah scream from the stable and the household began to stir. First out the door was Jane with the shotgun leveled at Tiller, followed by Martha, Cynthiana, and Laney. Aunt Lizzie came up behind the men who had gone to retrieve Big John and Sarah.

Aunt Lizzie waved a rag in the air and hollered, "Put that girl down. Put her down, I say."

Sarah kicked at the man who tried desperately to keep her under control. The other man led three horses, one of them Big John. Lottie could see Big John's eyes were wide and calculating. At this point, he had gone into self-preservation mode. She hoped he didn't kill anyone today. It wouldn't be the first man he stomped to the ground. While he did whatever Lottie wanted, there was wildness in him that she could never tame.

"Well, well, they come out of the woodwork. Look, boys, there's enough for all of us and some to spare." Tiller laughed and spat on the ground. "Now girl, we can take this horse and leave real peaceful, or we can tear this place apart. Your choice."

"There isn't one of you that can ride that horse nor take him against his will. I'll bet a silver piece to that fact." Lottie reached into her pocket and pulled out the only silver coin she owned.

Tiller's men laughed and poked each other, all indicating one man in the group.

"Go on, Bill. Get that money."

Tiller spat again, "If Bill cain't ride him, he cain't be rode. That's going to be my money and my horse. Go get 'im, Bill."

Bill was a tall, skinny man of about twenty-five. He moved lightly, like a cat. He stepped over to Big John, who had not yet had his saddle removed. He looked into the horse's eyes and spoke softly to him. Big John settled down and allowed Bill to mount and get seated comfortably. Lottie would later swear Big John winked at her just before he launched Bill a full ten feet in the air with absolutely no warning.

Tiller and the others were distracted enough to allow Lottie and Jane to close in. In one swift move, Lottie rounded the front of Tiller's mount and stuck her pistol in his gut. Jane stepped up to the man who had just let go of Sarah. Lottie saw her little sister spit part of the man's shirt out of her mouth. That left one on the ground not covered, and one mounted behind Tiller. Bill lay in the yard moaning.

Big John reared up, scaring the man who led him from the barn. He dropped his pistol and narrowly avoided Big John coming down on his head. One left. The man behind Tiller leveled his rifle at Lottie's head when a shot rang out from the elm covered yard. Out from the shadows stepped brother James and his two young sons, all armed.

"You gentlemen best be getting down the way. My sisters are meaner than snakes and been shooting since they could walk. You'd be safer away from here."

"Put your guns down boys and mount up. If you would be so kind as to have your sister here remove the pistol from my navel, we'll be on our way. Sorry for the misunderstanding."

Lottie stepped away from Tiller's horse but kept the pistol cocked and aimed at his chest. Jane followed her captives every move with the shotgun. James and his boys set their sights on the rest.

"We'll be going now."

The last to rise was Bill, who stumbled toward his mount and rose with a great deal of pain into his saddle.

"Wait, I believe you owe me some silver," Lottie said, addressing Tiller.

Tiller dipped into his vest pocket and picked out a silver coin. He flipped it into the air, but Lottie didn't reach for it and let it thud onto the muddy path. She kept the pistol and her eyes trained on the men as they moved off slowly, back from where they had come. When they had passed out of sight, Lottie lowered the hammer on the pistol and let out a sigh.

Jane comforted the frazzled Sarah, while the boys looked after Big John. James walked up to Lottie and placed an arm around her shoulders.

"Little Sis, I do believe you are going to kill a man before this war is over. Men like that will give you every opportunity."

"They'll be back, and they aren't from the army like they said. They're horse thieves. I saw them in the swamp. Said his name was Tiller."

"Patrol's been looking for a man named Tiller. Heard it in Goldsborough today."

Lottie bent to pick up the coin, saying to James, "Thanks for lending a hand."

She cast one last look down the path where the riders disappeared and shivered. Tiller would definitely be back.

Chapter Eight

March 22, 1865
Bath Day

On Wednesday mornings there were more chores than on other days. Tonight the family would load up and head out to the church for Wednesday night prayer meeting. These meetings were the only means of communication and were the lifeline of families and fighting men. More information was dispersed at prayer meetings in the South than at the army camps on the same night. Under the watchfulness of so many eyes, friend and foe alike made clandestine plans. This war had turned neighbors against one another. Genuine friends were a blessing and a necessity.

Lottie had just slipped her boots on when she heard the screen door on the back of James's house open and close three times. Lottie stood and held a stretch for as long as possible, relishing the feeling as the blood rushed throughout her body. Pulling suspenders on to overburdened shoulders one at a time, she stepped down to the yard, transferring a cup of steaming coffee from hand to hand.

James sniffed the air. "Ah, that smells amazing."

Lottie picked up the cup she had brought out for him. "It's real coffee, from Brazil, compliments of Jacob."

James took the cup and sipped cautiously. He breathed out a fog of hot air, with an appreciative sigh. "I had forgotten how coffee tasted."

"Brother, the wind is gusting strong this morning. It's driving that smoke up from the southwest. I'd say the Yankees had themselves a few bonfires going."

Lottie's nephews followed their father with sleepy steps, until the mention of Yankees, which caused their eyes to widen as they searched the horizon.

"Don't worry boys. You'll see your share of Yankees before this is through. Go on, get your chores done so we can have some breakfast."

James was stern with his boys but delighted in them. He raised them alone since his wife died of typhoid, coming up on five years ago in July, same batch of bad air that took Jacob's wife. Lottie thought those boys were the only reason James Edwards remained alive. They were his reason for being.

He smiled as he tussled his youngest boy's hair and spoke to the oldest. "Nathan, make sure your little brother here doesn't fall asleep in the hayloft before breakfast."

"Yes, Pa. Come on Ethan, if we hurry we might get breakfast before the Yanks get here."

Ethan, a beautiful, gentle boy of barely twelve, and his just turned thirteen, stocky, farm-boy brother, Nathan, were ordinary young men anywhere in the world heading out to do chores. Except, they both carried rifles. Ethan's gun was longer than he was tall and while it struck such a comical image, it was terribly distressing. As young as they were, Lottie's nephews were older than some fighting in the war.

"You keep an eye on Nathan, James. He has that look when he talks of Yankees. There is no need to lose him to this lost cause."

James replied, "I'm doing my best to keep them both out of it. It is getting harder to keep Nathan home, with so many of his friends donning uniforms of older dead brothers or fathers and marching off to war. It all sounds so romantic to a young boy."

At that moment, Sarah came bounding out the kitchen door with a steaming biscuit in her hand and Aunt Lizzie on her tail.

"Girl, you wait for your breakfast like all the rest."

Aunt Lizzie swung the ever-present rag in Sarah's direction, but the redheaded child was too quick for her.

"I'll be back for more after chores, this is just a warm-up for the main course." Sarah giggled and ran toward the chicken coop.

"Feed 'dem chickens and bring me some water, you triflin' chil'."

Lottie and James began to laugh but stopped as Aunt Lizzie turned on them.

"An the two of you needs to be gittin' on, too. I ain't holdin' breakfast for fools who can stand around laughin' at folks when der is chores to do." With that pronouncement, she turned and stepped back up into the kitchen mumbling about folks funnin'.

The screen door on the back of the house opened and out came Cynthiana, a dark beauty, who took after their mother. She was seventeen and quite sought after. She was dainty, but not fragile. Delicate was not a Bratcher woman trait. Delaney or Laney as she was most often called, followed Cynthiana. At fifteen she was stuck in between girl and womanhood. Laney was going to be a great beauty, but no one could convince her of that in these awkward years. Martha Ann closed the door behind them and went directly over to Lottie.

Martha Ann was shorter than the rest of the Bratcher women. She was plump and pink with strawberry blonde hair. Her face glowed with excitement.

"I had another dream. I am more positive than ever that Jefferson is alive and well. I saw him so clearly, there, by the smokehouse. It was just a shadow, but who else could it be? I tried to raise the window to tell him he could come in, but I only frightened him away. The dream was so real, I feel as though I have not slept."

Lottie cautioned, "Don't be so sure of your visions, Martha Ann. There are plenty of strangers wandering these swamps."

"I suppose you are right. Dressed all in black like that, it wasn't clear who it was. I assumed it was Jefferson because it wasn't the right build to be my Avery. It looked more like you, Lott. I don't know now, maybe it was a woman, but it just felt like I knew him and I thi—"

Lottie cut off Martha Ann's monologue. Anxious to change the subject, she inquired about their mother. "Did the herbs help Ma with the headache?"

The ruse worked and changed Martha Ann's course.

"Ma is some better. The medicine seems to help. I'll see if Lizzie can muster some broth for her. She'll be better if she eats a bite."

James gazed out over the swamp and plowed lands surrounding them. He said, "Ladies, these woods are full of thieves and bummers now. We have to gather what we can and hide it, or we'll starve come winter. I think the Yanks will have enough to keep them busy closer to town, so coming out this far will take a day or two. Lottie and I have been plannin' this for a time now. We got a flatboat hid in the swamp and been puttin' supplies back as we could."

Lottie nodded to her sisters. "I got a place, but I cain't tell you where for your own good. You cain't tell what ya' don't know."

Delaney spoke, "You think we'd tell a Yankee anything?"

"You don't know what you'll do with a knife at your throat," Lottie said with all sincerity. She wanted them to be scared.

James continued, "Sisters, let us turn our attention to the needs of the day. My boys are going to dig a hole under the smokehouse, just like everyone else. We won't finish it, but it will look like we were tryin' to hide the stores. We'll take off most of the meat, leavin' enough for them to steal. Dry goods the same. We need some of those new seedlings moved out to the meadow on the other side of the stream. Maybe they won't go out that far, and we'll have something to replant after the Yankees are done tearing up the place. In any case, we need to move the seed stores. Anything you value must be moved tomorrow. No big things, just what we can carry on a flatboat or horse."

The group broke up and went about the chores of the morning. Lottie attended to some loose boards in the corncrib. Slipping down to the mill shed, Lottie would come back and forth with materials and tools. She appeared to be doing chores. No one would notice the little items she removed from the crib. The family did not have much, but what they did have had meaning.

The most important single object was the deed that recorded Philip Bratcher's purchase of the land on which Lottie stood, dated 1803.

When she still spoke to her father, he would say, "Lottie, the land is all there is. They can't make more of it. Better hold on to what is yours."

Lottie had removed all the necessary papers to the safe haven of the Appletree Swamp hideaway months ago. Some folks believed in boxes kept in banks. Banks burned down. The swamp and a thousand-year-old stone quarry would still be there when all the fighting was said and done. The emerald belt of wetlands between Wayne and Greene counties held many pre-colonial secrets and more than a few recent ones.

Just after the sun rose above the horizon, the large bell in the backyard clanged the call to the morning meal. For an hour and a half, Lottie had been downwind of the kitchen, and the aromas made her stomach growl loudly. It always seemed when she ate as well as she had yesterday at Jacob's, she awoke more hungry the next day.

Aunt Lizzie stood at the back door of the house, inspecting the shoes, faces, and hands of Sarah, Ethan, and Nathan. There was no need to examine the older siblings, as they had learned that cleanliness was next to godliness in Lizzie's eyes years before. Lottie scrubbed a little harder at the pump with the knowledge that Lizzie was lurking near the door.

Aunt Lizzie had attended the birth of every child there. She had been with Parthenia, as a gift from her paramour, since the birth of her second child, Jefferson. Parthenia made it understood she did not believe in slavery, but the thought of leaving Lizzie with Harriet sealed both women's fates. Parthenia gave Lizzie her freedom on the first day, but Lizzie refused to take it. Her husband was on the farm next door. She'd have to leave if she was set free. The two women were bound by the love of each other and the love of men they never could quite have.

Lizzie's family had a small house on the property and worked alongside the rest of the Bratcher clan. They shared in feast and famine. Aunt Lizzie was as black as night, scrawny looking, but tough as a man twice her size. Her hair was always neat as a pin and her clothing spotless. It was a sense of pride with Lizzie that she could cook a full meal and serve it in a pristine apron.

As Lottie passed into the house, Lizzie questioned her, "When's the last time you had a proper bath, and not no dip in the creek, neither? Ain't right for a woman to dress like a man and bathe like one too."

"I will take my usual bath this afternoon with the rest of the ladies, thank you," Lottie said this playfully, and the old woman swatted her on the buttocks as she went by.

Lizzie called after her, "Before you wash, come let me put a' egg and some flax oil in yer hair for dem frizzies. I got one I can spare t' help with dat rats' nest."

Breakfast passed with idle chitchat about the war and the coming crop, the news of Charlie's return, and all that transpired in Goldsborough the previous day. Martha Ann tried to share her visions with anyone who would listen, but even the children had grown weary of her fantastic tales. Jane and her husband, John Simpson, came down to breakfast with the rest of the family. Jane brought baskets of what appeared to be items for the household, but was really the last of the belongings she intended to part with.

John Simpson was a sad case, to be sure. He had been a handsome, fun loving, hard-working young man. Now, he was just a shell, his insides taken flight, leaving nothing but bones. The doctor said there was always hope. Lottie wasn't so sure. She could see the shadow of the horror he must have seen in his cold, vacant stare.

After breakfast, the dishes were taken care of by Jane and Martha Ann. Cynthiana and Delaney finished the household chores. Chamber pots fell to Sarah, who complained loudly about the abuses of the youngest in the household. Ethan and Nathan, along with Thomas and David, Lizzie's sons, were directed to start the fires under the water tubs for the bathing and haul water up from the stream. With so many to clean, lots of water would be needed.

Brother went back to repairing farming equipment that had been passed down to him by his grandfather. Kept in good working order, these plows and tools would last forever. To keep them from the hands of thieves, James planned to pull the bulk of them over the stream and into the thick woods near the meadow. He'd have to leave something for the thieves to take, and choosing what to offer up occupied his mind.

Lottie let Big John and Jake out in the corral. After yesterday's incident, she wanted to keep them close. She went to the stable, grabbing anything she could and still leave enough to continue living and convince the thieves of the pitiable plight these women had been left in.

Truthfully, these women had continued to plant and attend to enough crops and stock to sustain a healthy lifestyle in comparison to some of their neighbors. With John Simpson barely aware of his surroundings and James being lame, the Bratcher women and children had maintained the farmhouse and outbuildings. Lottie was proud of her sisters. When the sickness at times took down their mother, who was an excellent source of courage and knowledge, it forced Lottie and her sisters to fend for themselves, and they had done so brilliantly.

All afternoon, preparations were made for the church meeting and the trip into the swamp. After a late lunch was served, the last of the chores were completed, and everyone took a turn either hauling hot water or getting a turn in the bath. Lottie was proud to have reached the age to start a new tub of clean bathwater, one that three sisters before her had not already used. The littlest and the dirtiest went last. Despite what Lizzie said about Lottie's bathing habits, she thought the creek and rivers a much better solution than the family bi-weekly ritual.

Everyone dressed in good clean clothes, but not their Sunday best. Wednesday church required only that one not smell like a field hand. Lottie wore a light cotton dress made of yellow and blue flowered print with a blue lace shawl over her shoulders.

Lizzie stayed home with Parthenia and John Simpson. Brother left a loaded shotgun with her. He placed a pistol on the table by John Simpson, just in case he might spring to life if needed. No one thought he would.

Jake pulled the wagon loaded with people and covered dishes for supper. Lottie sat with her knee around the horn of Big John's saddle, her skirts draped ladylike over her legs, so as not to expose too much skin. She left her riding boots at home, opting for button ankle boots. The weathered planter's hat had been exchanged for a simple bonnet.

Jane looked up at Lottie, "Why, Lottie, you almost look civilized."

Lottie resisted the temptation to remove the pistol concealed under her skirts and show Jane just how civilized she was. She instead clucked to Big John and led the Bratcher family up the north path toward Eureka, for the Freewill Baptist Church bi-weekly meeting and monthly church supper.

Chapter Nine

Prayer Meeting

Jonah Stancil, the Freewill Baptist preacher, greeted each neighbor as they headed into the one-room structure used for school, church, and community meetings. Benches faced forward on both sides of a black pot-bellied stove in the center of the room. Tall windows lined the walls to let in natural light.

"Sparse attendance for a supper night," James said.

"People are too afraid to leave their homes," Jane said. "Come on girls, let's get these dishes to the tables."

Most of the families present were Lottie's closest neighbors. There was the Barnes family, very wealthy slave owners with thousands of acres at their disposal, along with the Aycock, Peacock, Holland, and Davis families, who were also affluent, but not quite as gaudily so. Then came the Bayley, West, Chase, Jones, and other small independent farm families comparable to the Bratchers. Sharecroppers mingled in with farm laborers. It was a healthy mix and represented all strata of society, except slaves. Christian as they claimed to be, they congregation drew the line at slaves.

Jack Cole and his sons, Gabriel, a chip off the old block at sixteen, and Patrick, Patrice's darkly handsome twin, accompanied the Cole women into the service. Lottie noticed Patrice when the Bratcher clan arrived and had spent every moment of the evening avoiding her, until now. The sermon on the evils of war and striving for peace had not much meaning as cannonading from Mill Creek could be heard. The congregation eagerly exited the stuffy building for the picnic on the grounds. Once finished with the meal the men moved over under a big elm, where Jack Cole was holding forth on protecting one's own.

"Men, we cannot count on the army to save us now. We all saw them high tail it out of Goldsborough yesterday morning. Bragg left us here to fend for ourselves."

Lottie had slipped away from the women and eased over behind James, who leaned against a tree. She listened intently and was so focused she did not see Patrice come up behind her.

"He seems to have found his calling."

Patrice's closeness startled Lottie, but she held her reaction in check. "Hush up. I want to hear."

Patrice reluctantly turned her attention to her father.

"Mayor Privett surrendered Goldsborough to the Ninth New Jersey about three o'clock yesterday afternoon. From what we gathered today, Schofield, Terry, and Uncle Billy himself will camp in the area for a few days, waiting for supplies. That puts near a hundred thousand Yankees in our backyard. The bummers started arriving last night and have been coming in a steady stream all day. They won't touch Goldsborough proper, but they will come out of the town to rob and steal. The patrol will be ridin' every night. We need volunteers. Me and my boys will saddle-up with any man ready to protect our homes."

Patrick looked less enthused than his brother. From what Lottie knew of him, Patrick wasn't much interested in hunting anything. He liked books and poetry. Rugged certainly wasn't a word Lottie would use to describe him. Sophisticated suited him better. It had to be his grandmother's influence. There wasn't anything cultured about Jack Cole.

James stepped forward. "Cole, are you going to do anything about that Tiller fella? He was by the house yesterday—tried to take Big John."

A ripple of laughter filtered through the crowd.

Cole answered James's question. "We think Tiller is hiding over by Black Creek. Hard to tell how many men he has, but we are steady looking for them. He's a horse thief, stealing from the army

73

and selling them back up North. Seems the army is not the only place he's looking for horseflesh."

"He's a killer, Cole," James added for emphasis.

A silver-haired man spoke up. "I worry 'bout the boys comin' home with no papers. Some of 'em just had enough of war. They'd be no good to any army. You patrol boys gonna hunt them down like they say?"

"Hell yes! I despise a coward," spat out Gabriel, Patrice's younger brother.

"That's fine talk for a boy ridin' the home roads with his daddy and sleepin' in his own bed at night," an anonymous voice said from the shadows.

Gabriel was young, but he was mean. "Come out in the open, coward. You'd be wise to watch your step."

"Home guard is a far cry from Cold Harbor," said another voice, closer to Lottie.

She scanned the faces, but could not tell who had spoken. Good, she thought, they might need some friends before this was all over.

"Let's not fight amongst ourselves," it was Preacher Stancil stepping forward. "I have been given assurances by Mr. Cole and the other leaders that this patrol will not be lawless marauders, but men of honor and the highest character. I have therefore given permission for my young sons to ride and hope those of you that can come forth in this time of need will do so. God will watch over us. Your willingness to do God's work will make you holy and keep you in his comforting hands."

Jack Cole once again gained control of the quieted group.

"The preacher is right. We will uphold the law. The law says deserters are to be given a trial. I assure you all deserters will be given their say and justly sentenced. We must remember those who have paid the ultimate sacrifice for the South and protect their property as if it were our own. Our most pressing thoughts are on preserving our homes and protecting our wives and children from the slaves set free by blue-coated Yankee Negroes."

Lottie saw a knowing look pass between Gabriel and some of his gang of worthless sons of planters. There in the horde was the red glowing face of Calvin Edwards. Lottie knew that Gabriel would never do anything without gaining something in return. She was sure that before long, Gabriel would be stealing as much land as possible from young widows unable to make a payment or meet the taxes on all they have left in this world. Jack Cole was just mean. His youngest son was pure evil.

A few more words of encouragement from the planters produced more old men and boys pledged to protect this corner of Wayne County. As plans were made for patrol groups, schedules planned, and leaders appointed, Lottie started away from the men, hoping not to have to talk to Patrice. Miss Cole showed no interest in the goings on under the elm tree and instead chose to follow Lottie.

Lottie thought to occupy the conversation with topics of her choosing.

"So, what did happen in Goldsborough yesterday afternoon?"

Patrice seemed pleased that Lottie was interested in what she knew. She skipped up beside her and reported.

"Around three o'clock Mayor Privett and Constable Murray rode their horses right out into the face of the Yankees waving a white flag. They had been chasing after the last gray-coat on horseback, who fired over his shoulder at them. The Mayor and the Constable were unarmed, but they rode right up to maybe a dozen Union soldiers. The soldiers took to cursing something awful. Privett just held that flag and calmly asked for the commanding officer. I did not think him capable of such bravery."

"And where was the home guard, hiding in the hotel, peering out the windows with the young boys?"

"Why, yes. How did you know?" Patrice smiled at Lottie.

Lottie looked away and continued to walk with no particular destination in mind. She had a need she couldn't name to put distance between her and Patrice Cole. Still, Lottie couldn't stop talking to her.

She asked, "Well, what happened?"

"A group of Union officers arrived, saluted the Mayor, promised to protect the town property, its women and children, and only take what the army needed in provisions. They then moved aside while what looked like half the Union army double-quicked it over the old stage road near Bissell's Mill. They whooped and hollered and then settled in about town. The officers are housed in the best homes. Provost guards have been posted. More of Sherman and Terry's troops started comin' in around dark."

"So it's done? No shootin' or burnin'?"

"It isn't over yet, Lottie. Johnston has retreated to Smithfield, but the end does look near with Lee forced out of Richmond and now Petersburg."

"Lord, I hope so. I am tired of war and killing."

"Your brother said that man Tiller was after Big John. Do you think he'll be back?"

"Yes."

"Maybe you need more than a one-legged soldier and some boys to protect you."

"You forgot about John Simpson. He's about as useful as any other man I see around here."

Patrice laughed. "I've always found your candor charming."

"Patrice Cole, what are you and Lottie Bratcher talking about so seriously? I would think with your Northern education and fine manners that swamp trash wouldn't interest you."

Delphia Lane and her friends swooped in on Lottie and Patrice like a mother hen followed by her chicks. She was almost breathless as she nonchalantly placed her hand in the crook of Patrice's arm. Claiming her property, Lottie thought.

"Why Lottie, what a beautiful shawl. Your mother does the best tatting in the county. I must have mother put in an order for the wedding, I'm sure the money would help."

Lottie flashed hot, but before she could speak, Patrice turned in front of her and faced Delphia.

"Dear, sweet Delphia. I'm sure you and your ladies in waiting could use some cider." She turned to Lottie, "Good evening, Miss Bratcher." Patrice smiled at Lottie and then escorted Delphia and her minions back up the hill.

James walked up to Lottie. He had observed the previous incident and must have perceived her mood from afar. He stopped just short of Lottie, as she turned and almost collided with him.

"Whoa, there. Is Miss Delphia Lane speaking her mind again? What little mind she has is so occupied with the wedding chapel, she hasn't got enough left to be talking aloud. Patrick will be sorry he made that pact with the devil."

"I don't think he made that pact," Lottie said.

"No, I don't imagine he did. Jack Cole wants that marriage for more than just social standing. Patrick is being sold off like a stud bull, in exchange for a prime piece of land next to his father's acreage."

Lottie laughed, even though she tried to stay mad. Brother changed the subject before she could get angry again.

"Some of the families are heading into the swamp with livestock and horses. You'll need to be extra careful that you aren't seen tomorrow."

"Nathan and Ethan should come with me. They'd be a great deal safer with Jefferson, and I need the hands on the flatboat. I'll have to ride Big John and pull Jake behind."

"I think that'd be all right. I'll get them ready tonight. You're leaving before light, I suppose."

"Be better that way. I can be deep in the swamp before the sun comes up. Still, I was hopin' Charlie would show up before I went."

"He'll show soon enough. Let's us be getting home. There's a mess to do before morning."

Lottie could hear Delphia's cackle as they loaded up and pulled away. Folks like Delphia made being a forgiving Christian difficult. She'd been nasty to Lottie since they were born, practically. They were too old now for Lottie to just deck her or put a bug in Delphia's hair. Their mutual dislike had grown to the point that Lottie, very unchristian-like, hoped the patrol was nowhere to be found when the Yankees came to Delphia's house. Maybe one of them would take her away. Good riddance.

Sitting sidesaddle, Lottie looked back at the crowded church steps to see Patrice waving frantically. She ran down the steps in an apparent attempt to stop Lottie leaving. Lottie smiled, hitched up her skirts, lifted her knee from around the horn and threw her leg over the saddle. She stepped into the stirrups, clucked to Big John, and left the Freewill Baptist congregation and Patrice Cole in a cloud of dust.

Chapter Ten

Let It Burn

They saw the blaze-orange glow through the trees before they made it into the clearing. Approaching from the north, they could easily see Lizzie's little house on fire. Lottie kicked Big John into a gallop and pulled up in front of the porch where Lizzie, John Simpson, Lizzie's boys, and Charlie Hunt all sat with stunned looks on their faces.

The new arrivals climbed down from the wagon and piled into the yard. They too took in the look of disbelief on the faces of the porch dwellers. It began to dawn on the yard people that the porch people were all staring at John Simpson, who stared into oblivion as usual.

Jane took control of the situation. "You folks going to just sit there and let Lizzie's house burn down? What in God's name are you sitting there for?"

"Let it burn."

All the yard people shifted focus to John Simpson, who had just spoken.

"John Simpson, have you gained your tongue and lost your mind?" Jane moved over to stand in front of her husband, who was seated on the steps holding a pistol in his hands.

"Leave 'im be." It was Aunt Lizzie who spoke. "He done a man's job tonight. Leave 'im be."

James sat down by John. He slowly removed the pistol from the stunned man's hands and spoke quietly to him.

"It's all right, John Simpson. I'll take over now."

Lottie dismounted and moved over to the edge of the porch where she could see Lizzie's house was burned almost to the ground. All that was left were the hot glowing ashes in a neatly groomed pile. Someone had tended the fire. Lizzie held a rag to a gash under her left eye. Noticing the ash covered faces of Lizzie's two boys a picture started forming in Lottie's mind.

The family gathered close, as Charlie leaned over the railing and relayed the story, while the fire crackled in the background.

"Near as I can tell, from what Lizzie and the boys told me, two men came here looking for a light-haired girl with curls who rides like a man. Seems you made quite an impression the day before."

"Dem two was wit dat devil man yestidy," Lizzie piped in, as Martha Ann tried to soothe her and checked on her eye.

"They tried to go in the house, and Aunt Lizzie there aimed to stop 'em. That's how she got that cut."

Aunt Lizzie chimed in again, "Your momma, bless her soul, come through that screen door wid da shotgun and blowed a hole in one of 'em right der where Martha is standin'."

All eyes locked on wet spots underneath Martha Ann's skirts. She stepped aside with a gasp. Something had been washed off the porch and steps.

"The other one took off 'round the house and ran into Lizzie's boys coming out of their house to see what the fuss was. He fired at them, so they ducked back inside. When he kicked the door in the boys had gone out the rabbit hole in the corner. I rode up just in time to see John Simpson there come out the back door of the main house. He met the man coming back out the cabin door and shot him dead to rights in the doorway. The feller fell back and fired his gun in the throws of death. He must have hit something, cause the whole thing set to burning fast."

"We started to put out the fire, but ol' John there says 'let 'er burn.' I followed him around to the front of the house. He never spoke another word, just went about getting that shot feller around to the cabin. I started to see what he was thinking, and we burned that building and those fellers. Aunt Lizzie put your momma back in bed, and the boys tended the fire. Me and John washed off the porch and covered the tracks we could see. I'm sure they got friends and them finding bodies here would be bad for all of us."

"You'd be right about that, Charlie. It is fine to see ya', but I don't reckon this is the time for a visit," James spoke up. "Them fellers have horses?"

"They're tied out back in the woods."

John Simpson sat perfectly still during the retelling of the events of the night. Jane sat beside him, staring at him like he was a stranger. As if to say the night's work had been done, John Simpson rose slowly and walked away toward his house. He didn't say a word, never looked back, just walked home. Jane excused herself and followed him.

James watched his brother-in-law walk away, "Well, I'll be damned." It summed up what everyone was thinking.

Lottie was already planning. "Nathan, Ethan go down, get the tack off them horses, burn it in there with the rest of the cabin. Leave the bridles. I'll need them later. If y'all see anything that can be tied to them two, make sure nobody finds it. Rake them coals good, knives don't burn, neither do buckles. Throw all the metal in the privy hole. Make sure it sinks. Nobody will ever find it there. Put their guns on the back porch. We'll take them to the swamp."

She turned to Thomas and David. "You two best come with us to the swamp. James, I reckon they'll be needin' some of the boy's clothes. You go on get what you need, we're leaving tonight."

Aunt Lizzie rose on shaky legs, "Go on now, boys. Momma will be fine."

"I need to change out of these clothes. Is Ma awake? I want to say goodbye."

Cynthiana was coming from the interior of the house and answered, "She's awake. She's asking for you, Lottie."

Lottie quickly changed out of the dress and replaced it with her riding clothes. Before fetching her boots from the back porch, she crept into her mother's room.

Parthenia Bratcher had been a beautiful young woman, but the last few years of hard living had taken the luster off that beauty. She was only forty-seven years old, thin, and scarred both in heart and body.

She was lying there with a cold rag draped over her eyes. The cloth had been soaked in a brew sent from Mary at the hospital.

"Are the medicines helping, Ma?" Lottie whispered. Loud noise and light were impossible for her mother to take when the spells hit.

"Some," came the answer.

"You did real good tonight, Ma. It's all cleaned up, and no one will ever know."

" 'Cept, the Lord. I do hope he will forgive me."

"Ma, the Lord knows you did what needed to be done."

"Yes, child, the Lord forgives." She was tiring, and her words were barely audible.

"I'll be goin' to Jeff now, Ma. I'll be back tomorrow."

"Shug, y'all be careful, and come back to me safe. Tell them boys to stay where they are until the Yankees move on."

"I will, Ma."

She kissed her mother's forehead and whispered, "I love you."

Parthenia's hand reached out blindly in the dark. Lottie grabbed it and held it to her cheek.

In a voice that betrayed her fears, Parthenia said, "May God ride with you, child."

Chapter Eleven

Maarch 23, 1865
Runnin'

William Bratcher, Parthenia's brother, came riding up out of the darkness, trailing four horses behind him. He made the Bratcher call, before proceeding too close. The call had been taught to William by his father Phillip and passed down through the generations. It sounded like a very lonely morning dove. Folks didn't come to this part of Appletree swamp unless they intended to. You had to let the residents know right off if you were friend or foe, especially now. You wouldn't want to get shot by mistake.

William, forty-five years old with graying dark hair, was a handsome man. People said he took after his father, tall and thin, but not too slim. Uncle William kept the figure of a man much younger. He had done his conscripted stint in the infantry and come out whole. He was a lucky man.

"Martha Ann told Marie at church tonight that you would be going in the swamp in the morning, and I figured these horses would be safer with you. Save them if you can, but don't give your life for 'em."

"I'll do my best by you, Uncle Will," Lottie assured him while wondering what else Martha Ann might have said.

William inquired, "What happened to Lizzie's place?"

James answered him, "Got the bugs in the wood mighty bad. Had to burn it, to keep 'em from spreading."

Lottie thought James was right smart to come up with that excuse.

"Well, I'll be, if that ain't Charlie Hunt standing there."

Charlie and Uncle Will clasped hands, as old friends do. They slapped each other on the back and went on about how they were glad to see each other.

Lottie began to grow restless.

"Any news from Goldsborough out your way?" She asked as a manner of moving things along.

"Anders boy came by this evening. Said the bummers were headed this way. Won't be long now. Your momma feeling any better?"

James answered, "She has up and down spells. She'll be back on her feet soon, I'm sure."

"That's good to hear. I'll stick my head in before I leave." He paused but wasn't finished. "Lottie, you're the best horsewoman or man in this county. Everybody knows it. They'll be looking for you if you stay gone long. Keep to normal, best you can."

"I'll only be gone one night. James can say I'm checkin' traps and trotlines. It isn't unusual for me to do that this time a year. And nobody knows Charlie is here to miss him."

"Glad to see you are taking them boys with you. They tell me the army is taking the near babes to service, both sides. Forcing them to work in the camps."

Uncle Will would keep them talking for hours. Lottie had to make a move.

"Go on in and have a cup of coffee with Aunt Lizzie, Uncle Will. Ma will be awake in a little while. It's coming on daybreak. We got to get while the gettin' is good."

"The Lord be with you, Lottie."

Uncle Will patted Lottie on the shoulder and dipped his hat to James and Charlie. He climbed up the back steps and into the house. All the packs were ready. Nothing left to do but go. Lottie called the boys over with instructions on stringing out the horses. She rechecked Big John's tack.

"Little more'n an hour before sun up. Take care of my boys, Lott. They're all I got left."

"They'll be all right. Take care of home, and I'll be back before you know it."

Lottie patted her brother's worried whiskers and winked.

He smiled at her. "What I wouldn't do to have back the confidence of youth."

His boys strode up with the horses. Nathan and Ethan were given the appropriate "you are men now" speech upon which each hugged their father like the boys they were.

"Keep your rifles clean boys and don't let your Aunt Lottie get in too much trouble."

Lottie clapped her hands. "All right, let's go. Get in the flatboat. I'll be on the north shore. Pole up to the fork. Keep real quiet, now."

She bounded up on Big John and tied one string of horses to his saddle horn. Charlie did the same on his mount.

"Watch that sister of mine. She doesn't know what fear is, yet. Not the way we do."

Charlie looked down at James, "I won't let anything happen to your family, James."

Charlie followed behind Lottie on the footpath leading up the south fork of Appletree Swamp. They had a bit to go before they would cross into the dense wetland and disappear from sight.

The extra room Thomas and David took up in the flatboat had made it necessary to build a small raft to pull behind it. This slowed the boys somewhat, but they were making good time because of the high water and the fact they were moving with the tidal flow. The moon hung low behind them, casting long shadows out in front of the little boat. When a cloud blocked the moonlight, the pitch-blackness of the night clung on refusing to break for dawn. They dared not use lanterns, forcing them to creep forward, eyes sweeping the darkness for danger.

After an hour of slow progress they came to the crossing, a shallow sandbar that led deep into the swamp. Lottie and Charlie drove the horses across with little difficulty. With the assistance of one of the horses from the shoreline, the boys would have to pull the flatboat and raft through the shallows, over fallen logs and stumps. The high water made it easier. Still too cold for snakes, this method was not as loathsome as it would be in May when the moccasins were most active. Together they trudged along until dawn.

At daybreak, Lottie climbed down from Big John. She left the others to rest and warm up, while she walked out ahead to have a look around. She and Charlie had seen signs of other travelers. Though they never spoke while moving through the swamp, they had signaled each other at every broken twig and horse's hoof print.

Charlie had not been in the swamp in eight years, so he stayed with the boys. Although he had played here as a youth, he told Lottie he felt a little out of sorts. It reminded him of war and try as he might he could not help looking for Yankees in every shadow.

"My mind is telling me there are no Yankees this far north, but that sixth sense I developed during my time in battle has the hair up on my neck. Something feels amiss."

Lottie had worn her brother's old deerskin pants over her own wool ones and tied her boots tight with the pants legs stuffed inside. Still, the water seeped in every crevice. It was ice cold and chilled her to the bone. Her breath blew out in short bursts of steam as her heart accelerated at every sound. She stopped two hundred yards from where she left the rest of her party.

"Get control of yourself," she whispered.

She took a breath, deep and slow, and then listened to the swamp. Looking back from whence she came, Lottie saw nothing but swamp. The boys were safe with Charlie. Her breathing came under control, and she listened intently for any sign of movement in front of her.

Directly ahead, the swamp became deep enough to float the boat and raft again. The boys would have to follow the stream around the pine savannah that rose up just on the other side of the stream. Lottie and Charlie would be exposed as they crossed this savannah. The tall pines and sandy bottom prevented undergrowth and brambles beneath the pole straight trees. Any other time this portion of the trip was a relief from the thickets and cypress bogs. Today it would be the most dangerous, as she and Charlie would be out in the open for more or less three hundred yards.

Lottie had been kneeling behind a tall cypress stump while she took in the surroundings. Satisfied that she heard nothing, she stood to go back to Charlie and the boys. That's when Lottie smelled the tobacco. Quickly registering the smell, she ducked back down. Only humans smoked tobacco. Someone was near.

When she looked back again, she saw that Charlie was creeping up on her position, low and slow, using the cypress knees like crutches for his injured leg. She cautioned him with a hand signal, and he hunkered down, pistol drawn.

There among the pines on the savannah, she saw four men dragging what appeared to be a very reluctant cow behind them.

When they were closer, Lottie heard one of them say, "Where in the hell are we, Jewel. We have been roamin' in these woods for an hour. I say we go back where we came from and don't never come back in here again. Ain't nobody gonna come this far in this swamp to hide nothin'."

"I guess you're right. Ain't nobody, but a fool gonna come much further than this. Let's go back where we found this cow and see if we cain't scare up some more. I swear people are fools, just turnin' their livestock out in the swamp so's the Yankees won't git 'em."

"It's divine providence, Jewel. The Lord will provide," said the one with the smoking pipe between his teeth.

They turned around and started back across the savannah.

The one dragging the cow said, "I hope the Lord provides for the patrol to get busy fightin' Yankees and forget about us hidin' out from the infantry."

The voices trailed off, and Lottie breathed a sigh of relief. They were moving on and had not seen her. She waited a few minutes before she moved and then fell back to Charlie's position. She explained what she had seen and heard. They decided to go back to where the boys were and eat a bite. They'd wait a while before moving on, just in case.

They spoke in whispers as they waited. Charlie wondered aloud about the broken trail they had been following.

"The trail looks fresh, maybe yesterday," he said.

Lottie agreed with Charlie's assessment but still kept her eyes steadily moving over the landscape. Whoever came in here, might still be here. Everyone was hiding things in the swamp, but not too many people came back in this far. Those men were lost and not from around here. The trail she had seen was deliberate and heading straight for Jefferson.

As soon as they felt safe, the group began to move toward the open water and the savannah. The boys listened carefully as Lottie gave directions for following the creek. She would meet them on the other side, she said, "and above all, don't make any noise."

Charlie and Lottie pushed the boys off on their way. They were frightened but excited. Little Ethan sat in the middle of the flatboat holding his rifle close to his chest. He looked back at Lottie and smiled, then continued his survey of the swamp, on guard.

"He's so young and so brave," Lottie said with an air of both sadness and admiration.

"And he'd be so dead if we left him with your brother. These bummers have killed a hundred boys like that. I've seen their handy work from Georgia through South Carolina. I've seen boys younger than Ethan hung over wells and dunked till they died. No one left alive to cut 'em down. He'll be safer with Jeff and me, they all will."

Lottie caught the tear on her cheek with her sleeve. She was surprised at its arrival. She hadn't even known she was crying. She wondered if the tear was for the boy Charlie spoke about or the lost innocence of the ones in the boat.

"Let's ride."

Charlie and Lottie thought it best to ride slow and make the least amount of noise possible.

Lottie rode a little behind Charlie, watching the muscles flex in his arms. Her eyes wandered to the back of his neck and paused on the ringlets of red curls that hung over his collar. She remembered the times as a young girl that she had dreamed of Charlie being hers. Her crush had nearly killed her when he moved away. She still loved Charlie, but it felt more brotherly than romantic. That crush was nothing compared to the longings Patrice Cole stirred.

Lottie realized too late that Charlie was looking at her.

Confident they were alone, he struck up a conversation. "Lost in thought I see. I said, what is all this with Tiller and his gang. How'd you get caught up in that?"

Glad for the distraction from thoughts of Patrice, Lottie explained, "I saw them coming home yesterday. They followed me. They tried to take Big John, and it didn't go as they planned. He said he'd be back and I believe he will. He scares me, Charlie."

"James said the patrol was looking for Tiller. Maybe they'll find him before you get back."

"That would be fine by me. There is pure evil in that man."

The rest of the trip across the savannah went without conversation. Coming to the water again, they dismounted and waited for the boys on the boat to come around.

Lottie pointed at what looked like a shallow crossing. "Can't ford here, though it looks passable. The bottom is a bog, and the horses just get stuck in the mud. That's the reason most folks don't mess around these parts. You can go around, but it takes another hour or so, depending on how high the water is."

Charlie climbed down from his horse. "How are we going get these mounts to the other side, then."

Lottie walked over to a clump of peat moss and debris under some trees. She started kicking the pile and uncovered a makeshift flat bridge. She had carried materials back here for almost a year before Jeff came home. She was making a place for the family to hide if it became necessary.

"There's a rope and pulley system on both sides to help pull it over. Jacob helped me figure the mechanical advantage. When the boat gets here, we'll set it up. Then we pull it over to the other side and reverse the process on the way back. It doesn't matter what side the bridge is on, it can be pulled out from either side. I try to keep it covered though."

"Lottie, you've thought this all out, haven't you?"

"There wasn't much to do but farm work, with Jeff gone and James wounded. I've had a camp back here since I was old enough to be turned out by myself—a place to trap and fish. I figured it would be smart to have somewhere to go if trouble came close to home."

"It's a shame you have to do the work of men. You are too pretty to be trapping and farming."

"Pretty still has to eat," Lottie reminded him.

"How did you get this far back in here to begin with?"

"My grandfather would come back here to get marl clay for the garden. There's an old marl pit on the other side of my camp. I've seen signs the natives were in here a long time ago, mining the clay for medicine, pottery, and fertilizer for planting. There's a quartz quarry back there too, and deep sand pits over closer to Green County."

Charlie shivered. "Them marl pits ain't nothin' to play around. I saw a big buck get sucked down in one. The more he kicked, the faster he went down. Wasn't long before the whole animal disappeared."

An awkward silence fell over them. Then the sound of poles tapping the side of a boat broke the moment. The boys were coming down the stream. Relieved to see Lottie and Charlie, the boys visibly relaxed when they came into sight.

After some maneuvering, the bridge was attached to a rope, pulled across the open water and made ready for the horses to cross. The bridge was just wide and sturdy enough for one horse to cross at a time. This took a bit since they had ten horses and Jake, who at first balked at the passageway, but moved on over after Big John crossed first. The bridge dipped into the water with his weight but held. That appeared to be good enough for Jake, and he moved on over with no more defiance.

Once all had crossed the bridge was pulled over and covered with peat moss, waiting for the next time it would be used.

Lottie told her party, "We're real close."

Everything from the boat and raft was loaded onto the horses. The watercraft was then taken upstream to a thicket Lottie had hollowed out for just this purpose. She removed a pile of dead foliage to reveal the opening, where they placed the boat and raft and covered them up. The rest of the trip would be on horseback. The boys seemed relieved to be off the water.

They came again to dry land where a wall of loblolly bay trees formed an impenetrable thicket before them. Lottie moved out in front and showed the others how to follow a path through the maze. Soon they entered a clearing. Looking back at where they had been, it seemed the path had disappeared.

"Nature's gateway," Lottie said noticing the boys' astonished expressions. "I'll show y'all how to find the path. Once you know, it's easy enough."

Lottie began the Bratcher call, which was answered shortly by someone very near. They had moved forward just a few feet when three scraggly, bearded, and armed men stepped out of the underbrush. The sudden movement frightened the horses, and the boys drew in their breaths.

The tallest of the three bearded men, with the eyes that exactly matched Lottie's, said in a husky whisper, "Good Lord, Lottie. Did you bring the whole county with ya?"

Chapter Twelve

Brotherly Love

"I'll be damned. Charlie Hunt. I thought we'd seen the last of you at Gettysburg. My God, brother, welcome home."

Charlie slid off the saddle and settled himself on his one sound leg. He and Jefferson clasped each other's forearms and stared into one another's eyes—the warrior's stare.

"I wasn't sure if I had really seen you that last night out there," Charlie said. "I thought maybe I dreamed you up. I wasn't thinking real clear at that time."

Lottie approached the two men with a broad smile.

"Thought you'd like some company. Found this ruffian over at Jacob's landing, hauling a whole passel of children and not a one of them his."

Jefferson kissed his sister on the forehead. "Jacob never said a word. He said you were bringing something special, but I never guessed it be this."

The group began to unload the supplies and stash them in the various holes and crevices of the giant cedar trees that surrounded the area. The camp Lottie had staked out was one of the few dry places this deep inside the swamp. It was an almost circular area of sand with a high flat spot in the middle. The sides sloped off at the edges where the trees and brambles formed what looked like impenetrable walls for almost the full circumference. One cleared area opened onto the water, which flowed a good five feet deep just off the shore. Long before Jeff and the boys arrived Lottie had prepared a fire pit, over which now hung a pot she recognized as the one Jacob had loaded into the johnboat two days ago.

There were makeshift lean-to's set up around the fire pit, with a sitting area of logs ringing the inside of what was now home to five of the South's toughest fighting men. They had seen so much blood and gore that even the quietness of the swamps could not silence the sounds. That's what Jefferson told her. It was the sound of war that haunted them in dreams and waking moments. They described the wailing of men burned alive in the Wilderness campaign, while their friends stood by helplessly lost and confused.

A thunderstorm brought the immediate terror of breathless moments, head down, the sound of "Incoming!" ringing in their ears. Lottie had gotten as close today as any time to war. It quickened the heart to hear the cannons firing miles away. How did these men lay there, faces in the earth, awaiting the order to charge, all the while rounds and rounds exploded around them? Lottie marveled at the men who sat around the fire, as the afternoon faded into evening.

Chores done and all fed, the conversation turned to battle as it always did when young men were about. Ethan, Nathan, Thomas, and David were no exception. They sat fixed in awe of the real-life soldiers with whom they found themselves bonded. The horrors of war had not yet faded their glory-filled notions of what killing meant. The men kept the stories light, steering away from fighting. They talked of plays the companies put on for one another and the endless nights of singing around the fires.

It was Ethan who asked the question, "Pa told us your being home is a secret. Why's that? I mean you all look like you're 'bout fought out. Why would they want to make you go fight some more when you done all you can?"

"That's an interesting question, son." Jeff sat back and chewed a pine stick.

Nathan looked at his uncle long and hard before he said, "You ain't no coward are you, Uncle Jeff? That's what the boys were saying 'bout the men who come home without permission."

"And they said the patrols would hang all the yeller bellies for sure," Ethan added as a matter of fact.

91

"That boy right there, Harper. He went in at seventeen years old in '62. He stayed with me through the whole damn thing. Never got a scratch. Then at Cedar Creek, he got hit in the leg. They took him to the field hospital. He was lucky because the bullet only hit flesh.

"They bandaged him up and sent him right back to the field to fight the next day, which he did. The fever was already burning him up, but he fought. He became delirious, but he kept fighting. I don't know that the fever didn't do something to him. That spot won't heal, and the flush comes on him now and again, taking him to his bed. He's been in that state for a week or more this time.

"He would have died out there, and he wasn't any good to his ma dead, so I brought him home. Harper ain't no coward, son. There's many a dead Yankee to testify to that. All us fought long and hard, but now them that's in charge are leading men to slaughter. Let us fight like we know how to, we said. Over and over again they lined us up and marched us into live fire. We just done enough of that marching into hell's valley, that's all. We done enough and we came home, while there was still a home to come to."

The other soldiers nodded. Lottie had read Jefferson's diary and knew how these men had come to be in this place. He had offered her the accounting of his war experience as a way for Lottie to understand why he came home the way he did.

Jefferson told her, "I can't stand to see doubt in your eyes, Lott. I need you to know I done all I could."

Four of the five men now living in Appletree Swamp had returned to active duty together on September 1, 1864, after being listed as "hospitalized."

Jefferson recalled in his notes, "It was no hospital. Soldiers lay on blankets thrown on the ground, where they either cured you or buried you. If you were strong enough to get up and walk away from the stench of rotting flesh, you did. We went back to active duty because the alternative was dying from a disease, laid up with all them sick fellas."

The other men came with their own stories. Eli Parsons had been wounded at Spotsylvania Courthouse back in May. Jefferson, injured that day too, ended up in the hospital with Eli. From that moment on, despite the six-year age difference, or perhaps because of it, Eli would not leave Jefferson's side.

Deland Smith and Joshua Garrett had been wounded at Gettysburg, held prisoner in northern hospitals for nine months, and then returned to the rebel army in Virginia. There they were moved from one hospital unit to another, finally meeting up with Jefferson near Bunker Hill. Twelve months in and around hospitals had taken a toll on Deland. He looked much older than his twenty years. Joshua fared no better, already a hunched old man at twenty-eight.

Harper Aldred, just a kid, was beloved by all in his unit. When he took ill from his leg wound, nearly crazed with fever, and was asked to charge once again, Jefferson called it quits and walked off the field of battle.

He wrote, "Up and down this same damn valley, going nowhere. We are about to be marched headlong into a superior force again. How foolish to line up and march at the one that is shooting at you. I am a hunter, not beef being led to slaughter at the whim of wealthy men. The Yankees have new repeater rifles. This is a butchering no man should be asked to volunteer for. On this day, November 11, 1864, I begin my travels home, in search of something that makes sense. This war never did."

That was his last entry. On the road for the better part of three months, Jefferson and his friends appeared as the walking dead in the fog at the edge of the woods in Bratcher Patch. Now, after some rest and ample food, gaining weight and strength, Jefferson had begun to resemble the young man he was before joining the army. If the patrol saw him now, they would wonder why a healthy man wasn't fighting. His smile and the blush of his cheek belied the battle scars under his clothes and in his mind.

When Lottie looked up from her thoughts, Jefferson was staring at her. She smiled back into the face that so mirrored her own. Folks had always commented on how she and Jefferson were cut from the same cloth. A silent message passed between their matching hazel eyes. Jefferson wanted to talk, alone.

The young boys began to ready for bed. In preparation for their arrival, the band of swamp dwellers had been busy building raised beds and shelters with the tools Lottie had brought them. The youngsters would be safe and dry and on an excellent adventure, which made up for any lingering feelings of homesickness. Besides, they were much more sheltered here than if the Yankees found them at home.

A breeze brought with it the soft thud of cannon fire in the distance.

"That's over near Black Creek," Jefferson observed.

The boys paused to listen and then scrambled for their beds. Wide eyes peeked from under covers, as Lottie passed them on the way to check on Big John.

"You're safe here, boys," she said, offering comfort to the youngest and most frightened. "Good night. Sleep well."

While Lottie brushed Big John down, Jefferson approached.

"I still don't know how you've held on to this horse. I guess no one wants to steal a horse he can't ride."

Lottie replied, "I damn near lost him the other night. That Tiller man I told you about, I fear him more than the Yankees in Goldsborough."

"Sister, I've never known you to fear any man, but I see a darkness over you as you speak of him."

"I tell you, Jeff, I see evil in his devil eyes. It chills my spine. I want shed of him and his kind. This war can't end soon enough."

"The end will only be the beginning for folks like us, Lott. The old guard knew where the working class fit in their world of aristocrats and social station. Now, the haves have not, and they'll be looking to us to get it back, mark my words."

"Jack Cole and Gabriel are out to get their share," Lottie commented.

"Stay clear of Gabriel. He's meaner than his father if that is possible. Patrice and Patrick aren't like the rest of those Coles. They take after their momma's people."

Lottie thought Jefferson might have had his eye on Patrice before her daddy shipped her and Patrick up north. Most of Wayne County's eligible bachelors did. Rumor had it Patrick was caught with a sharecropper's son doing something "ungodly," as Jane had put it. No one really knew the truth.

Lottie thought Jefferson had mooned over Patrice going away. It wasn't long after that he went over to Bullhead and then on to Guilford County. Jeff seemed to wander a bit before the war, unable to put down roots.

Lottie thought that she and her brother were probably both in love with Patrice, which couldn't be right and certainly wasn't going to come to anything on Lottie's part. It was just another reason for hating Patrice to add to the list. At the mention of her name, Lottie changed the subject.

"How's Harper's leg? Did you pour the water over the dogwood and give it to him like Medicine Mary said?"

"It didn't help as much this time. I put the horsemint oil on that hole, but it's still feverish. That leg has to come off. There ain't no way around it."

Lottie didn't like that idea. "Out here? You want to take his leg off in the swamp? He'll die for sure."

Jefferson shook his head. "No, not out here. I think I should take him on to the pickets in Goldsborough. The Yankees got themselves a nice hospital set up by now, I reckon. They will take him prisoner, but at least he'll be taken care of. The war won't last much longer, and he'll live to see his momma again."

"But what about you? They'll make you a prisoner, too, or shoot you on the spot."

"Not if I tell them I want a blue coat and a rifle."

Lottie was shocked. "You would do that, Jefferson? You would switch sides?"

"There isn't a side to this war, Lott. These are rich men's battles fought on fields littered with the bodies of less fortunate men. We were conscripted for something most of us don't believe in. The sooner we end this folly, the sooner we stop the killing. I'd wear a blue coat to make that happen."

Lottie's mind raced. Jefferson smiled to ease her worries.

"Besides, I would really like to get out of this swamp."

Martha Ann's words came to Lottie. She narrowed her eyes at her brother. "You have been out of this swamp. Martha Ann saw you in the backyard."

Jefferson looked genuinely shocked. "It wasn't me, I swear."

"Well, somebody has been coming back this way. Charlie and I trailed them near to your door. You better post two guards from now on. Everybody is running into the lowland. Sherman doesn't have anyone left to stop him. Raleigh will fall soon."

95

"Lee can't hold out much longer. To do so is inhuman," Charlie said, joining them from the shadows. "The Constitution has held. We will return to the Union and our manifest destiny."

Jefferson's previously darkened countenance brightened. He smiled at Charlie, saying, "You still read too many newspapers, Charlie Hunt."

"I may be a dirt farming hick, Jefferson, but I'm a learned one. Thus far, I have lived to tell of what I know by remaining one step ahead of a silencing bullet."

Lottie burst out with, "I'll take Harper to Goldsborough. We'll stay one step ahead of the Yankees and the patrols. Jacob can take him by boat to the landing. I'll meet him there in my Sunday best, and tell them he's a wounded man sent home by the Rebs because they are losing and can't take care of their own."

Jefferson stopped smiling and jawing with Charlie instantly. "You will not, Charlotte Bratcher. You have already done more than you should."

"But what if Jack Cole finds you? Gabriel isn't going to be waiting to hear any man's side of the story like Jack claimed they would. They are fired up to hang every deserter they find at home."

Charlie snorted a laugh. "Isn't it ironic that they are home, objecting to others trying to get back to their own?"

"Ironic or not, Gabriel Cole will kill me on sight. Lottie is right."

"If you want my two cents, I think it's a solid plan," Charlie commented.

Lottie sold the idea with, "I'll take Uncle William's mare. I'll leave Big John with you. They are looking for him and a girl dressed as a boy. The Coles don't operate that close to Goldsborough, so if I make it to Jacob's with no trouble, then all I have to do is convince the Yankees to take Harper to the hospital or to let me do it. That doesn't sound so hard, right?"

Chapter Thirteen

A Friend is Watching
March 24, 1865

"Shh! Someone is out there," Lottie whispered to James.

She took a step back into the shadows and stared down the hill, beyond the creek. A series of gusts shook the trees. Lightning flashed behind billowing clouds, revealing a thunderstorm building off to the east. When things quieted down again, Lottie was sure whoever had been there was gone.

"I think we have an unwanted guest living close by. I'm telling you, this swamp is crawling with people I've never seen before."

James puffed on his unlit pipe, for want of real tobacco. "Times are desperate, Lott. We don't have much, but we have some. That's more than a lot of people can say."

Lottie remembered the hopeless faces of the fleeing throngs on every path out of Goldsborough. "Charlie said he saw awful things on the march. He warned not to be too kind to strangers these days."

"So far, whoever it is hasn't taken anything that we have missed."

Lottie corrected him. "The sisters said someone milked the cow before they could get out to the meadow this morning."

James laughed. "Oh, yes. The great milk theft. Sarah was distraught. She brought ol' Bess back to the barn for fear she would be stolen."

"Did you explain that is why we took her out of the barn?" Lottie asked, chuckling quietly.

"Sarah would listen to no argument and vowed to sleep in the meadow if we forced her to."

"That child has an unusual relationship with our farm animals."

"She learned it from you, Lott."

"So, who is milking our cow and wandering around the yard in the night? Do you think it's Tiller's men?"

James shifted his weight on his one leg and adjusted his crutch. "No, I don't think so. I'm leaning toward our milk thieves as the source of the shots that ran Tiller's crew off last night. I could have sworn I heard two pistol reports nearly simultaneously. There could be more than one person out there."

"How many of Tiller's men came last night?"

"I saw three," James answered. "Could have been more."

"And the shots scared them off?"

"One of them swore and yelled to the others that the patrol had found them. That's the first time I've ever been glad to see Jack Cole ride out of the shadows."

"How do you know it wasn't Jack's boys that fired the shots?"

"Because that's what drew the patrol to us. Jack said they heard the shots and came to investigate." James pointed down the hill and beyond the creek. "They rode off after Tiller's crew, leaving us to wonder who was hiding in the woods out there."

Lottie dipped some snuff into her lip and offered her brother a pinch.

"How do you manage to always have snuff, Lott, when no one else does? What's your secret?"

Lottie grinned. "I plant some tobacco every summer, way out in the swamp on a savannah. I cure it and make my own snuff. I traded some of it to Mr. Wahl for supplies. I have to keep it on the sly so it won't get confiscated for the army."

"You can keep a secret better than any woman I know, Lottie Bratcher."

"I figured if I told anyone, including you and my lovely sisters, the word would get out and I'd be pestered to provide for others. I share, don't I?"

"Yes, and you gave me a pouch every year for Christmas. I thought you traded Mr. Wahl for it and it was the other way around.

Well, I'll be dogged. You are a devilishly clever girl, to be sure. The man that marries you will need a superior mind and a strong hand."

One of Lottie's eyebrows rose in a questioning arch. "The man that would try a strong hand with me would fail your first stated requirement."

"Point won," James said, with a chuckle.

Lottie went back to the reason they were standing behind the old barn.

"As I was sayin', Charlie and I kept seeing trail sign. I asked Jefferson, and he said it wasn't him. I had just crossed my makeshift bridge coming back this morning when I heard a child cry out. I found two grown women and their five babes hiding in the weeds, not a child with them more than six years old. The women turned out to be sisters with a strange story."

"How the hell did they get back in there that far?"

"That's what I asked them. One of the sisters said they had moved in together because their menfolk were gone in the war. They were sharing an abandoned shack over by Faro because they couldn't farm the land they were sharecropping without the men around and got run off from their homes. Some men came to the shack—"

Lottie hoped the darkness would cover the tears she felt falling. Nevertheless, the pause was indication enough for James. He hugged her to him. Lottie relaxed into her big brother's chest, but could not quell the anger continuing to rise. She pushed away to rant between clenched teeth. The fact she couldn't express how she felt above a whisper deepened her rage.

"They took that tiny girl, James. They did things to her. These men are not Yankees. They are local men who think they can do as they please with this war on. Men like Tiller don't all come from far away. We have an abundance of our own monsters."

"How did the women end up in Appletree Swamp?"

Lottie wiped away the tears with the back of her hand. "That is the part I don't quite have a handle on. Loretta, that's the oldest sister, said a man and woman found them sitting outside the burned-out shack and told them they would be safer in the swamp. They were taken to where I found them and told to wait there for the next guide. That's who they thought I was."

"So, you took them to Jefferson?"

"I didn't have much choice, James. I couldn't leave those children in the swamp. I wasn't sure if the people would really come back for them. We had already run into a couple of thieves out there the day before."

"And they had no idea who the rescuers were?"

"None, but Loretta, the youngest sister, did say their rescuers said there were a lot of women and children living in a village in the swamp and that's where they were being taken."

"I've heard that all my life, about runaway slaves living deep in the swamp. Ika-arwee, that's what they called the place. Grandma said that was Tuscarora for Moon-Water. That could be made up too, just like the mysterious village."

Lottie nodded. "I've looked for it myself. I think everyone that ever heard that legend has a theory about where it is. Jacob said he has searched for it too. How could it exist then? He knows every piece of open water in Wayne County and these swamps better than anyone alive."

James spat a stream of tobacco juice into the darkness.

He said, "Even Jacob will tell you he gets turned around over by Contentnea Creek. Besides, Jacob can keep a secret as good as you can. He wouldn't tell us if he did know."

Lottie spat off to the side, having once had a bad experience with a wind gust and an attempt to match James in distance.

"You're probably right, Brother. I suppose we should get some rest. I have a long day tomorrow."

"I'm going to ride with you to Musgrave Crossroads, just to see that you're on your way safely."

"I'll enjoy the company," Lottie said, surveying the darkness one last time. "Let's get inside. I can't shake the feeling of being watched."

"You are being watched," a female voice said from the back porch.

James leaned heavily on Lottie's shoulder and his crutch, as they approached the two shadowy figures on the porch. Jane handed Lottie a folded black dress and cape, with a hat to match.

"The hem has been let out. It should fit you well. I still think this is a ridiculous idea."

"I can't let him die, Jane. I have to help him."

"Why isn't his family helping him?"

Jane wasn't easy to convince, but Lottie had thought her story through.

"Old Mrs. Adler is all that is left of her family, besides Harper. She can't make this trip. Jacob can only take him so far."

Jane huffed. "Pigs will fly before the Yankees take a sick Rebel into a hospital."

"Have faith, Jane."

Jane stepped off the porch. "Come on, John Simpson. Let us take our leave." She addressed Lottie and James, "Good evening and God bless you both, even if I believe you mad."

John Simpson passed close to Lottie and slipped her a piece of paper. He then joined his wife and disappeared into the darkness.

"What does it say?" James asked as he followed her to the oil lamp in the parlor.

Lottie unfolded the note and read, "A friend is watching. You will be safe on your trip. Enter the city at John Street picket."

James smiled and nodded. "There is a lot going on in that man's head. I really can't much blame him for remaining quiet. If I was married to Jane, I might go mute too."

"That's true," Lottie said while looking out the window. "But I don't think he wrote this note."

"Why do you say that?" James asked.

"Because John Simpson doesn't smell like roses."

Chapter Fourteen

Our Country Cousins
March 25, 1865

"Sir, may I ask why you have stopped before reaching the picket?"

The Yankee officer's eyes traveled quickly over the wagon. He slowed his observation when he reached Lottie, who held the reins.

James smiled up at the mounted officer.

"Yes, you may ask, and I will tell you that I have delivered my scoundrel sister into the hands of the Yankees and will now return to our home to mourn her fate."

The officer's eyebrows shot up in surprise. "Why, what has she done?"

James feigned despair. "She has offered herself to help with the sick and wounded enemy. She does not believe in the cause." He leaned out of the wagon, closer to the officer, adding conspiratorially, "I think she may have her heart set on marrying a Yankee."

Lottie laughed and spoke for the first time. "My brother is a bit histrionic. Officer, would you be so kind as to help him with his horse?"

James swung his stump toward the stunned blue coat.

"What shall I do?"

James instructed, "Just bring her alongside me here. I can do the rest."

The officer followed orders, and soon James took his seat in the saddle of his prancing mare.

"That's quite an impressive display of upper body strength, sir," the officer said, "but I'm still in need of an explanation for your travels."

James took the crutch Lottie held out to him and tucked it in a custom holder he built for the purpose. "Sir, I told you true. My sister has forsaken the cause and joined the Union."

A female's laughter nearly jarred Lottie from her portrayal of innocence. She looked around the officer for its source, knowing exactly who it was.

Patrice and Patrick Cole sat on two magnificent chestnut mares enjoying James's show.

Patrice spoke to the blue coat. "Lieutenant Andrus, are my country cousins entertaining you this morning? They certainly are charming, aren't they?"

The Lieutenant doffed his hat in Patrice's direction. "Good morning, Miss Patrice, and you, Mr. Cole."

"Yes, Lieutenant, it is a gorgeous Carolina morning," Patrick said. "Put down your sword and come let us tempt you with sweet muscadine wine, while you regale us with stories of bravely surviving this insanity thus far."

Patrick's smile hid so many secrets, Lottie thought. One could never quite tell if Patrick were genuine. He seemed to wear masks of interchangeable expressions to fit his needs. It was also unnerving how closely the twins resembled one another. Sometimes Lottie thought she loved them both, which meant she hated them equally.

"Brave doesn't stop bullets," James said, as his horse pranced in a circle. James's weight discrepancy from the missing limb still had an unsettling effect on the animal. The mare's rider paid no attention to the anxious strutting. "Dumb luck is the only thing standing between the Lieutenant and a hole in the ground."

Lottie waited for the officer's response. James should have left the talking to Patrice. The Lieutenant appeared to have been struck dumb in her presence.

Exactly when Lottie thought she could wait not one more second for the Lieutenant to speak, he said, "Mr. Cole, if your invitation extends to this evening, I should hope to find you waiting in your parlor at the downing of the sun."

Patrick's smile grew into a wicked grin. "That you shall, Mr. Andrus."

Lottie soon found herself on the other side of the picket, waving farewell to James. Solving one problem led to another. Now Lottie wondered how she would rid herself of the Cole twins. She had the nearly three miles to Jacob's landing to formulate a plan. Luckily, the road was too narrow to ride abreast. Lottie followed behind the Cole twins. Uncle William's mare pranced in her harness, keeping pace with the horses ahead without being asked to do so.

From this view, Lottie had time to study the twins. That black as night hair, a thick braided rope hanging down the center of Patrice's back, did not come from the redheaded Cole clan. The twins' mother, Eliza, was said to have worn the same straight black hair wrapped in a braided halo around her head.

Lottie had asked about the twins at dinner. They were on her mind when everything else wasn't.

"The Cole twins look a lot different from the rest of that family," Lottie blurted out.

Jane, the family know-it-all, eagerly explained, "Eliza, their mother, was a Cane before marriage, said to have come from a Tuscarora bloodline."

Wayne County had once been home to a vast native tribe. After years of warfare, at the turn of the century, the remainder of the Tuscarora returned to upstate New York. A few, like the Canes, intermarried, assimilated to the white man's ways, and prospered. By the early 1800s, the Canes were wealthy landowners, which was probably why Jack Cole courted the beautiful Miss Cane.

"Ma said there was no more fine-looking woman in North Carolina than Eliza Cane and Jack Cole had to have her," Jane disclosed. "And of course, with Eliza's hand in marriage came her share of the Cane naval stores fortune."

Made from tapping the sap of the plentiful Long Leaf Pines, the coastal plains of North Carolina led in the production of tar, pitch, and turpentine since colonial days. The sailing industry required tar to keep ropes and sail rigging from decay, and pitch prevented leaking. Turpentine had a variety of uses on land and sea. The Canes cashed in on that demand.

Jane's telling of the Cole tale had not ended. She continued, adding a twist, "A sudden illness wiped out all of Eliza's male family members shortly before the wedding."

"Convenient for Jack," Lottie commented.

"Eliza and her mother survived because they were visiting Richmond on a buying trip for the wedding. Rumors flew about the cause of the deaths. A cook was questioned, but nothing came of it. They found them all dead with an empty carafe of Apple Lady, after a night of whatever men do alone in parlors. It was the end of the Cane male bloodline."

Jane's recounting told that the wedding moved forward, the twins were born, and people forgot about the mysterious ailment that killed four healthy men. When the twins were five, Eliza died. No one knew what killed her. She took sick and passed within hours, the same as her family before her. Eliza's mother also became ill but hung on the precipice of death for months until regaining her strength. She lived another eleven years. She built that fine new home in Goldsborough, where the twins have taken up residence since returning. Jack remarried, had Gabriel with his new wife, and people forgot about the strange killing ailment.

James added to the story. "When Eliza's mother passed, she left her entire fortune to the twins with the restriction that Jack Cole could never profit from a penny of the Cane estate. If anything happens to the twins before they have heirs, it all goes to the girls' seminary."

"People say that's why Jack sent the twins away. He was fit to be tied over that will," Jane said.

James slid his empty dinner plate away and stared at Jane. "You really don't know? Jack doesn't care for Patrick's particular brand of charm. He beat Patrick near to death over a rumor about a sharecropper's son. He would have killed him had not Patrice interceded on her brother's behalf."

Lottie asked, "Why did they come back here? I would have killed a man who beat a brother of mine that way."

"Who knows," Jane said. "Maybe they've come back to get even."

"Patrice said they were poor now too," Lottie said.

Jane waved a hand at Lottie dismissively, "She's got more money in a shoe box than I'll have in my lifetime."

The Cole twins were two years older than Lottie, making them twenty, soon to be twenty-one if memory served her correctly. Lottie tried, but could not remember a time when her infatuation with the Cole twins did not drive her to distraction. At community gatherings when they were small, all the children played together without knowledge of social status. Lottie had not yet experienced the stigma of being a concubine's daughter.

Only when she understood the circumstances of her birth did Lottie turn away from Patrice. The landed gentry would have no use for the castoff children of rich white men. Lottie excluded Patrice from her life before the Cole twins could inform her that she wasn't worthy of existing in theirs. She may not want anything to do with Patrice Cole, but Lottie couldn't face the thought of being rejected by her.

In Patrice's presence, Lottie felt reason leave her. The physical reaction confused and frightened her. She could actually feel the heat rise to her face as the blush flushed her skin. Her heart quickened its beat. Her breathing became short and shallow unless Patrice's fragrance wafted through the air. At the first hint of her scent, Lottie couldn't help herself. She breathed deeply, taking Patrice in. No matter how badly she wished to be shed of her feelings for the dark-haired beauty, Lottie's body remained defiantly devoted to Miss Cole. Young Miss Bratcher had thus far found forbidden desire a formidable temptress. She was about to be tested again.

The road widened, allowing Patrice to drop back beside the wagon. She seemed almost giddy to be speaking with Lottie, as if they had joined together on a grand adventure. "At this pace, we should reach the John Street picket in a bit less than two hours," she said.

"You are free to quicken your horse's strides and arrive before me," Lottie replied. "Your 'country cousin,' slow as she may be, is capable of finding her way and not in need of an escort."

Patrice laughed easily. "The Yankees believe us all inbred. Why not use their ignorance against them?"

Lottie challenged Patrice's nonchalance. "You seem friendly enough with that officer."

"Lott," Patrice used a pet name, one reserved for family and the closest of friends.

This caused a fluttering in Lottie's heart with its implied intimacy. How could that be? Patrice merely said her name.

"Lawd, have mercy," Lottie whispered, self-chastising and yet forgiving of her weakness for this woman.

Patrice asked, "What did you say?"

"Nothing. You were about to defend your cavorting with the enemy."

"Oh, yes, I was saying that I don't have an enemy in this fight, but if I did, it wouldn't be the soldiers of either side. My trouble is with men in general. They have yet to evolve beyond killing one another as a means to solve disagreements."

"I suppose I'll have to agree with you on that front. I have to know, why did you come back here?"

"I told you. We ran out of funds."

"You are heir to a fortune. How is that possible?"

Patrice grimaced. "I see the rumor mill has reached Bratcher Patch."

"You aren't heir to a fortune?" Lottie prodded.

"Yes, and no. Yes, but this war brought blockades and trade prohibitions. The shipping industry has found other ways to gather what they need. The forest is over-tapped. It now takes thousands of trees to produce what a hundred would. Kerosene is taking the place of turpentine-based illuminants. We set the slaves free and used what money we had to move them up north by steamer. Grandmother put our trust money in a New York bank, which we can't access until we are twenty-one. There are a lot of reasons I have little and take what I can from anyone on either side, but the main one is the war."

"You set the slaves free?"

"I couldn't go on owning anyone. We couldn't pay them with the business foundering. It was the right thing to do. Patrick agreed."

"So you're an abolitionist. I had not noticed a red string on your lapel. A member of the Heroes of America, are you?" Lottie asked.

"One doesn't have to be from the Quaker belt or a member of a secret society to believe human beings should not be owned."

"Shockingly, we agree, again."

107

Patrice smiled down from the saddle. "I knew we could be friends, Lottie Bratcher. I've always known that."

"Don't get ahead of yourself," Lottie warned.

"I do believe this is the longest conversation we've had since you were fourteen. You have avoided me since I moved up north. Each time I returned, your tone grew more terse. I've wondered why that is, Lottie. I want to be your friend."

Lottie longed for this exchange to end. She also wanted to talk to Patrice for hours, endless hours. It was indeed a conundrum.

"I suppose I have to talk to you," Lottie explained. "Apparently you have been roaming about Bratcher Patch at night, delivering notes through a mute man."

Patrice's expression was one of genuine surprise. "What on earth are you talking about?"

Either Patrice knew nothing about the note, or she was a great actress.

"The note," Lottie said, "it came on stationary that smelled like you—uh, I mean, that smelled like roses."

The corner of Patrice's mouth twitched into a fleeting grin, before she said, "Many people have rose water stationary, Lottie. The Wahl Brothers donated reams of it to the girls' seminary to write letters home for the wounded. I'm sorry to ruin your fantasy, but I've not been slipping around Bratcher Patch in the darkness sending you clandestine notes. What did it say, this note you thought I sent? Did I confess my love for you?"

"What about your brother, Patrick? Where was he last night?"

"My brother's comings and goings are no concern of mine. Unless, of course, he is a romantic interest of yours. That would complicate things."

"Why?"

Patrice fumbled a bit, "Uh, well, he's," before she grasped an answer, "because he's engaged to Delphia."

Lottie snorted. "Ha! How can he stand to be in the same room with her?"

Patrice laughed too. "He avoids that circumstance whenever possible. I know he wasn't with her last night. I had to deal with her insufferable whining because she could not locate him."

"Does that mean you do not know where Patrick was?"

"No, Miss Bratcher, I do not know, nor could he vouch for my whereabouts. Alas, your suspect list grows."

"Does Patrick ride with Jack? The other night at church, he stood with Jack and Gabriel. Yet, you say you are not on any side. Does he feel the same way? I don't understand your leanings. What are you two playing at?"

"My family seems to be a great concern of yours."

The sun peeked over Patrice's shoulder. Lottie squinted up at her. "My family is my concern. I can't risk being involved in whatever you and your brother are up to."

"Lottie, please believe me. I would never put you or anyone you love in danger, but you already are. Beware, you have no idea who your friends are."

"Or who they are not," Lottie added.

Patrice looked over her shoulder and then back down at Lottie.

"I'll see you soon. You'll be okay until you get to the picket at John St. Wait there. Someone will come for you and the boy."

Patrice clucked to her horse and trotted up to join her brother.

"Wait, how did you kn—"

Within seconds, Lieutenant Andrus rode past and joined the Coles. The horses quickened their pace under the three riders, as they began to pull away from Lottie in the wagon. Patrice glanced over her shoulder before rounding the curve ahead. By the time Lottie made the turn, the riders were out of sight.

"Good," Lottie said, trying to convince herself she was glad Patrice was gone.

A hundred yards up ahead, Jacob's landing waited. For the rest of this leg of the trip, Lottie tried to make sense of what Patrice seemed to understand but denied she knew. Was the note from the Coles or someone else?

Lottie also wanted to know why her body seemed to vibrate in Patrice's presence. She had infatuations before, both male and female idolizations. There was nothing unusual or wrong about loving a female friend. Her older sisters and mother told her it was innocent and natural, a part of learning how to love and deal with a broken heart. Lottie didn't tell them why she asked the question.

Her mother and sisters did not need to know about the French postcards with the women on them, the ones she found after the Yankees passed through in the first year of the war. At first, Lottie couldn't look at them. A glimpse was all she could bear. Slowly she began to study the women and what they were doing to one another there in black and white. The cravings conjured by those images were never quenched after that and being around Patrice made it so much worse. What Lottie felt inside—the glowing, the overwhelming want of physical touch, the fantasies that came in the night—she presumed was not included in the innocence of a crush her mother and sisters had described.

Lottie spoke to the mare because no one else could hear her. "I don't think I should be thinking these things or feeling those things, but Lord help me, I have no idea how to make it stop."

Chapter Fifteen

Pigs Do Fly

"Damn Yankees. They're everywhere."

"You picked a fine time to wake up," Lottie said to Harper.

He flopped back down—unconscious again, she hoped. Harper had roused a few times at Jacob's while being loaded into the wagon. The fever made him believe things only he could see, but this time he was correct. There were Yankees everywhere, in the woods and on the paths, swarming like bees.

Stantonsburg Road became clogged with people trying to enter and others trying to leave Goldsborough. Starting miles outside of town, the roads thickened with soldiers in worn uniforms. Most trousers had no material from the knees down. Lottie saw not one regular soldier in a jacket that retained both sleeves. These were Sherman's men. They were in the process of taking timber from the surrounding woodlands to build, Lottie assumed, some sort of encampment.

"I suppose they plan to stay," Lottie said to Harper, though he was no longer listening.

She glanced back to see that his head remained on the saddle she brought along. Lottie didn't want his head banging about the floor of the buckboard on the rutted out road. In this case, she was glad Harper looked so near death. She was more than likely to be believed when she said he was done fighting and in need of immediate help. Lottie raised her eyes to the surrounding land and spoke to her patient.

"Harper, there are thousands of Yankees, spread out as far as you can see. God help us, if they decide to kill us all."

A legion of black faces spread out across the land, at work for the Union army. Some wore the blue uniform of a soldier, but most were in rags, having followed Sherman's army out of the slave-holding deep South. They were the US Army's to deal with now and apparently no one knew what to do with a black man except work him. When she arrived in Goldsboro proper, Lottie imagined she would find groups of black women cooking and doing laundry for the troops. Slaves may have been given their freedom, but the Union had given, it appeared, no forethought as to what would happen to a people dependent on the system the abolitionists destroyed.

She commented to Harper, though she knew he couldn't hear her. "It seems the northerners do not mind making free laborers out of Negroes, so long as they don't call them slaves."

A cheer went up in front of Lottie. She heard it greeting the steam whistle of an arriving train. If it was moving south of Goldsborough, then it was carrying Union supplies. What army doesn't love a quartermaster's train? The bluecoats in front of her picked up their pace, double-timing it through the picket line.

Lottie slowed the wagon at the approach of a soldier waving his arms in the air, about a mile and a half outside of town. He cleared the road of non-military traffic. The rest of the travelers had to wait. When he neared Lottie, she smiled and appeared as hospitable as possible to the stranger in the blue jacket. Inside, she prayed silently that she and Harper didn't end up swinging from a rope.

"Pull to the side and wait here, ma'am," the soldier said.

He glanced into the back of the wagon at Harper, but made no comment and moved on to direct the next carriage off the road. Lottie held the sigh of relief. She let it out slowly, while her smile remained like the marble lips of Diana. This next part would be the hardest. Lottie had to pass through the pickets with a wounded combatant in her care. What could go wrong?

Waiting there, while squadrons of men marched back into town with foraged timbers, Lottie observed a massive line of earthworks going up as the forest was coming down. There wasn't a tree left standing between her location and the town. Lottie could see not just the steeple of the girls' seminary, but the entire building and surrounding lot filled with tents and wounded, all of which would have been invisible from her observation point yesterday. In addition to the deforestation, the landscape now had tents and shelters built over every inch of ground. Above the aroma of open-fire cooking, the pong of smoldering wet cotton hung in the air. That wasn't all Lottie smelled.

Humanity, foul smelling and unwashed, left its scent like a cloud over the city. Adding to the malodorous veil were the rotting bodies of dead horses, mules, and other farm animals within Lottie's line of vision. A little dirt had been tossed over them, but it did nothing to dent the stench. She imagined there were many more in and around the town. These animals were confiscated, driven from their stables by the conquering army, and then discarded when they were no longer of use, left to starve or killed outright. Lottie had grown used to man's inhumanity to man, but the mistreatment of an animal she could never stomach.

Refugees shuffled along, so covered in dirt their monochrome gray made race and social standing tough to distinguish. Antebellum ladies of the ball walked with babes in arms, toddlers clutched at the knee. Some trailed servants, who knew nothing else but to follow the mistress. Neither party had a home anymore. The Union believed "total war" would be required to end this one. The slave owner needed to feel the lash, understand the pain of want and need, be stripped of all that made them feel superior to the law of the land. Lincoln's men would preserve the Union at the cost of scarring her forever, and in so doing, prove no man above the law.

Lottie read an article in a newspaper James brought home before Sherman's march through the south began. In it, the General had said, "War is the remedy that our enemies have chosen, and I say let us give them all they want." Now, on the opposite side of the road, young children in the remnants of matching velvet suits joined a woman wearing what was once an expensive opera cape in digging through freshly dropped horse manure. Lottie watched as they unabashedly gobbled down any under-digested corn and oats.

Lottie said to her unconscious traveling companion, "I believe Sherman was true to his word. These folks have had all they could want of war."

"State your business."

Lottie turned her attention to the uniformed man at the head of her horse. "I have a sick man, here. I need to get him to Dr. Davis at the seminary."

With all the gold braids on his shoulders, Lottie assumed he was an officer. He gave her a good looking over, before continuing around to the back of the wagon. Lottie prayed Harper would remain unaware of his surroundings.

"He's feverish. He mostly just sleeps. He doesn't know where he is when he wakes. That leg has to come off."

The officer looked at Harper's leg and waved a hand before his nose to disperse the smell. "I'd say it might be too late for this one. Who is he to you?"

"A family friend. His mother is too old and feeble to make the trip. He's all she's got left."

"Leave him here. We'll see to it that he gets buried proper." The officer waved at two of his men. They came toward the wagon. "Remove this man," he ordered them.

"He needs a doctor," Lottie objected.

"So do a lot of men in blue. This rebel is done for. We save those we can."

"He's a farm boy that needs to be around to take care of his family," Lottie countered.

"He's a reb soldier with a festering bullet wound. I'll not take a bed from one of my own to give to this grey back. Your entry is refused. Go home, girl."

The men reached for Harper, who started to stir. The frustrations of four years of war, the waste of human life, the destruction of what had been a troubled, but happy existence, all of the pain and sorrow Lottie experienced in recent years exploded out of her.

"No, I will not go home!"

She hopped over the seat and into the back, a bit quicker and with more athleticism than the men expected. They stepped back from the wagon.

"Harper Adler will see a doctor, today. I'll be sure of that," Lottie said. "I didn't come all this way to leave him on the side of the road to die. We regular folks didn't have a say in how we ended up in this war, but we'll have a say in how we go out of it. This boy isn't going to die here today if I have to drag him over that corduroy road inch by inch myself. I've had enough of killing and dying. This boy is going to live. Do you hear me?"

"Brava, brava, Miss Bratcher," a male voice said behind her. "I echo your sentiments."

Lottie turned to see to whom the voice belonged. All the men within hearing distance snapped to attention.

The officer who told Lottie to go home said, "General, sir," and saluted.

The mustached man he saluted said, "As you were."

Lottie saw then the chestnut mare and its rider, Patrick Cole, just behind him.

"Good afternoon, miss. I am Brigadier General George Dodge, chief quartermaster. My friend Patrick explained who you were as we approached during your most impassioned speech."

Lottie nodded and acknowledged him with, "General."

"If you pardon me a moment, I would like the honor of escorting you and young, Harper, is it?" Lottie nodded again. "Yes, then, I should like to escort you and young Harper to the hospital, where he will receive excellent care."

"Thank you, sir," Lottie said.

Patrick winked at her. He and his sister looked very much alike, but not identical. Their facial expressions, however, were indistinguishable, the smiles especially. Lottie couldn't decide if she liked Patrice because she reminded her of Patrick or the other way around. It was a confusing way to enter the world of romance and sexuality, especially when she had no idea exactly what all that entailed.

Troubled and recovering from the blush of anger that caused her to hop into the back of the wagon in the first place, Lottie climbed over the seat. She gave no thought to the drawers she exposed to a crowd of men who had clearly not seen clean, white undergarments on a woman in years, at least not for free. They gawked openly as Lottie readjusted her skirt and hat.

"That's what I like about you, Lottie," Patrick said, as he moved closer. "You do not mind showing your petticoat if it will get the job done."

"Are you inferring, Mr. Cole, that I'm a fancy girl?"

"Oh, no. My comment was not meant as an insult. I honestly admire your blindness to social norms when they get in the way of necessity."

The General interrupted Lottie's exchange with Patrick. "Now, Miss Bratcher, I have to ask, is this man a deserter?"

Lottie hesitated to answer.

Seeing this, Patrick explained, "An order has been given stating that a Confederate deserter coming within union lines is to be paid for the arms and equipment he turns over, required to take the oath, and will be allowed free passage within the lines. Young Adler can come into town, if when he awakes he promises to be a good boy."

Lottie smiled with relief. "I imagine when he wakes with one leg, he'll have more to worry about than fighting Yankees." She turned to the General. "Yes, he left his line, sick and dying, back in November. It took him a bit to get home, but here he is, such as he is, half-dead. I promise you he'll take the oath of allegiance to the Union when he's in his right mind again."

"There is one other provision, Miss Bratcher. Your young man will not be permitted to re-cross the line. He will remain here in Goldsborough for the duration of our stay here in your fine city."

"I don't imagine Harper will be in a hurry to get back to breaking his back on a farm, sir, especially since he will have to learn to do it on one leg now," Lottie said.

General Dodge chuckled. "Your honesty is most refreshing, Miss Bratcher. And now, may we escort you through the line?"

"Yes, thank you."

Harper chose that moment to sit up and take a slow look around. He turned to Lottie with wide eyes.

He raised a finger to his lips and whispered, "Shhhh. I think they got us surrounded," after which he immediately passed out.

Chapter Sixteen

This Bloody War

On the day Sherman entered Goldsborough there were two-thousand-eight-hundred-and-eighty-eight sick and wounded already on hand. After the last of his troops arrived on the twenty-third, it took until near nightfall of the twenty-fifth to place all the injured and ill in beds. The Wayne Female College, already acting as a Confederate hospital, became a Union hospital and took on the wounded from the surrounding battlefields. All of the hotels, boarding houses, and selected private homes were turned into hospital wards. In as far as the number of tents would allow, wounded men were placed under canvas in every open space around town. Others were housed under the roofs of local citizens.

Goldsborough, a city under siege, had been trampled. Not a fence post remained. Even the outhouses had been torn down and used for firewood. Dead horses swelled with rot lay everywhere. The town had taken on the odor of death. Cotton bales, black with soot, littered the streets. From a fourth story window of the girls' seminary, Lottie saw the still smoldering railroad depot and the glowing embers of the freight storehouses on Center Street. The citizens of Goldsborough couldn't blame the Yankees for that. Jack Cole and his gang set it ablaze just before the blue army arrived.

On the way to the hospital, Brigadier General Dodge explained that upon learning Sherman himself intended to bring his troops into Goldsborough, General Schofield ordered the Provost

Marshall's office to supply guards to anyone wishing to protect their homes. Bluecoats stood guard outside the homes Lottie could see from her vantage point. There appeared to be a small garrison around Bass's store over on Ash Street.

"Men at war find a need to display a mask of civility. Among all this chaos, we're granted white-gloved men to guard the front doors of a conquered people," Lottie said, her breath fogging the window glass.

"Your cavalier behavior belies the depth of your thoughts, Miss Bratcher."

Lottie turned to find Dr. Davis lighting a pipe behind her. He puffed several times rapidly, drawing the flame of his match down into the bowl of tobacco. Most everyone she knew used tobacco in some form. Lottie left her snuff with James. It was the last of the batch. When he let out a cloud of smoke, Lottie thought it was the first time she had seen a genuine smile on Doc's face in years. She missed her snuff more.

"Ah, real English pipe tobacco, courtesy of my new Yankee doctor friends. Speaking of friends, yours is doing well. He kept the knee, which will make his life easier. If he lives through the night, he'll do fine. Got to get that fever under control."

"Thank you, Dr. Davis. I know he's in better hands now. He made it this far. It would be a shame to lose him now."

"The boy is a fighter. That's half the battle, the will to survive."

Outside a bugle began to play.

Dr. Davis saw Lottie's puzzlement and explained, "That's the 'Retreat' ceremony. The soldiers will turn out for the lowering of the flag at sunset. 'Reveille' sounds at sunrise. Later on tonight, you'll hear 'Tattoo,' which signals time for the soldiers to bed down and secure the post."

"I will not be around to tuck the Yankees in. I'll be at Jacob's by then, and home before dawn."

Dr. Davis's expressed surprise. "You cannot leave Goldsborough once you have crossed the line. You will need special privilege, a paper allowing you to pass the pickets. You will not be going home this evening. You'll need to see the Provost in the morning."

"The hell you say," Lottie said. "I'll go through the woods if I have to."

"What woods?"

Lottie's head snapped around at the question, which came from the stair landing.

Patrice came forward, asking again, "What woods? The forest has been stripped bare out nearly five miles now. If they haven't made it to Jacob's landing, they will soon enough."

The Patrice that approached Lottie was unlike any she had experienced before. Her hair was covered with a muslin cloth tied at the back like the washerwomen downstairs. A few stray coal-black strands stuck to her perspiring brow. Her skirt was hemmed six inches too high. The sleeves of her blouse were rolled up past the elbow. The bloodstained apron and stockings added a tinge of horror to the ensemble.

Dr. Davis addressed her, "Miss Cole, you have been here since the early afternoon. Please take your leave before the streets become the playground of scoundrels."

"I shall be on my way. I've come now to fetch Miss Bratcher." Patrice focused on Lottie. "Come with me. You'll be safe in my home, but we must be going."

Faced with a flight or fight situation, Lottie chose to resist Patrice. "Aren't you entertaining Lieutenant Andrus? Shouldn't you clean up some before he arrives? I can take care of myself, as I've told you before. You run along and prepare for your evening."

Patrice laughed. "I assure you, the handsome Lieutenant isn't the least bit interested in me. Oh, Lottie, you have so much to see beyond Bratcher Patch."

Dr. Davis chuckled. He patted Lottie's shoulder as he walked away saying, "Listen to her, my girl. Eyes wide open."

Lottie's chest swelled a little, and her pride showed itself. "I am not a child, nor am I a country bumpkin."

Patrice tried to calm her. "No one is suggesting you are either."

She smiled in an attempt to disarm Lottie, who saw it as the ploy it was and still could not fight off the charm. Patrice must have seen the physical change in her opponent because she continued her comment.

"I am suggesting that there are places and people out there, beyond Appletree Swamp, that you must see. Things I could show you if you'd let me."

119

"Why do you insist I need your charity, Patrice? Am I one of your missions? Free the slaves. Save the wounded soldiers. Educate a poor forest wench."

Patrice leaned against the stair banister. She looked tired, which was incongruous with her laughter. "Lottie, you have stretched my imagination, but I have never fancied you as a wench."

Lottie began to chuckle too. "Barmaid wench is a stretch for me, do you think?"

Patrice nodded. "May I begin again? My approach was heavy-handed, and I can see you are not one who appreciates being told what to do."

The hardening of her defenses against Patrice had failed. Lottie began to give in. She knew it was happening, and though part of her brain warned against it, Lottie relaxed her guard against adoring Patrice Cole.

"Please," Lottie said, "explain my position. Are you saying I cannot leave Goldsborough tonight?"

"No, the pickets close at sunset. I will help you secure a travel pass out in the morning. You will be safe, warm, and well fed at my home. Would you do me the honor of joining me for the evening?"

As calmly as she could, because her insides were turning cartwheels, Lottie said, "I suppose my choices are quite limited. Please, lead the way."

Foul odors, moans, and screams permeated the air. Lottie had a new appreciation for Patrice, who moved through the chaotic milieu with grace. She smiled and spoke to soldiers who called out to her. She stopped to hold a hand or wipe a brow too many times to count. Patrice had known most of these men for only moments, but they also were drawn to her like moths to a flame.

All the way down to the second floor and out onto the portico, Lottie studied Patrice; how she seemed to float above the dreadfulness, shoulders steady and steps light. Patrice wore no caged crinoline under her skirt. It hung naturally down to mid-calf over a shortened petticoat. After crossing the second floor to the exit, while holding her skirts above the blood and dirty water, Lottie understood why Patrice's skirt was hemmed short. Lottie longed for the boots and trousers she preferred over corsets and petticoats.

"Patrick took your mare and wagon to the house already. They will be safe there in the stable. We have an officer staying in our home. A guard is posted."

"Your leaving Wayne County is a foregone conclusion, then," Lottie said.

"Why do you say that?" Patrice asked, looking back over her shoulder, as she descended the staircase to the ground.

"You opened your home to a Yankee. I agree with your views, Patrice, but befriending them will earn you no peace when they are gone."

Patrice reached the bottom of the stairs and twirled to face Lottie who followed. "We have only a lowly Lieutenant Colonel in our home. We asked for General Sherman, but alas, he preferred the immense and quite lovely Richard Washington home. Do you think they'll run the richest man in town out on a rail for cavorting with the enemy?"

"I suppose you had no choice," Lottie said, feeling a bit naïve for misunderstanding.

"No, we did not. If the Yankees left our home unmolested, then that would be cause for suspicion."

The clamor of horses moving fast drew the attention of everyone on the campus grounds, including the two guards at the base of the steps. They raised their rifles, ready for a challenge. Down Oak Street came two riders followed by a wagon loaded with wounded men. They did not stop until they reached the base of the stairs.

One of the guards asked, "What happened?"

The soldier on the lathered lead horse jumped down from his saddle and explained excitedly, "We ran up on some vigilante patrol over near a place called Bullhead. Ran 'em up on some big spread."

The second guard asked, "Did you catch them?"

The soldier still on horseback said with a smile, "Yeah, we caught 'em. Some got away, some got dead, and we brung one to Uncle Billy for a prize."

Patrice and Lottie stood at the base of the stairs, not speaking, as men gathered around the wagon and began carrying the wounded into the seminary.

Finally, Lottie spoke, "Were any of the vigilantes wounded? Were they left to die out there?"

The horse soldier turned quickly, red-faced and spitting mad. "Do you know who these cowards are? If you do, tell us. We'll put an end to this madness, this mistaken belief that the South will rise again. You're done for." He raised his voice and shouted to anyone in earshot, "You're done for. If we have to hunt through every house and corncrib, we'll find you. End this bloodshed. Give up, before you force us to burn you all out like lice. You're done for, hear me! Done!"

A cheer went up on the grounds. In the dusky shadows, no one could tell if only the wounded and sick northerners shouted out their support. Lottie suspected many of the rebel soldiers leaned out of their bunks to join in.

"We are all so sick of war," she said.

"Then bring your menfolk to quarter," the soldier barked.

"My menfolk are limbless or too sick to fight, so they have been removed as obstacles to your endeavors," Lottie answered, a might too sarcastically.

The soldier raised his arm, as if to slap her, but was interrupted by a prisoner being escorted from the wagon in shackles. He was bloody from head to toe, barely able to stand. One swollen eye shut under a distended brow matted with blood-soaked hair. He drooled a crimson stream from cut and mangled lips. Only his right eyeball remained recognizable as human, as it rolled about, seeking a friend. It settled on Lottie.

"Lottie, they killed him. They killed Pa."

The soldiers jerked Calvin Edwards, or what was left of him, toward the stairs.

"Pa is dead. They burned us out," Calvin yelled, before a soldier punched him in the stomach, ending his ability to speak further.

The angry soldier glared at Lottie. "Do you know that boy?"

Lottie looked up at the soldier. She felt Patrice move closer and squeeze her hand. She glanced one more time at the staircase, as Calvin was led away, and then returned her attention to the soldier ready to pounce on her.

Her tone less truculent, she answered, "No, sir. I don't know him. He must have mistaken me for someone else."

"Ah, Captain Fleischer, I see you've met my sister and our cousin."

122

The captain was unmoved by Patrick Cole's insertion into the conversation. He asked, "What's your cousin's name, Mr. Cole," without taking his eyes from Lottie.

Patrick stepped between the two women, placed an arm around each, and pulled them close. He smiled and winked at Lottie.

"Why, this is Charlotte. And a sweeter lass you'll not find unless you cross her. Then she's a bit of wildcat with a biting wit."

"Charlotte, huh? Do you call her Lottie?"

"Sir, Lottie is what we call the housemaid. Now, I must be getting these ladies home. The darkness will overtake us as it is. Fine ladies are not to be caught out after dark in these uncertain times."

"You be sure to keep them there, Mr. Cole. There are enough gray backs running about tonight."

With their backs to the seminary and at an even pace, Patrick led the two women across the expansive lawn to the carriage waiting on William Street.

"Breathe ladies. Now, you should find me amusing and charming."

Patrice smiled at her brother and laughed. Lottie played along, laughing with her.

Patrick leaned toward his sister and whispered, "Jack is alive. Gabriel is missing. Preacher Stancil's boys are dead, and two more from over by Eureka were shot through." He then turned to Lottie. He kissed her on the cheek and smiled for anyone who might be watching them. "Everything Hub Edwards had has been burned to the ground."

Lottie did not think that she would care, but she did. She asked, "Is he really dead?"

"He ran back into the main house after it was set on fire. The roof caved in moments after. No one saw him come out. My condolences, Charlotte."

Lottie's throat tightened. She swallowed emotions she thought long buried and forgotten.

Patrice left Patrick's side and moved to Lottie's. "I am also sorry for your loss." She slid her arm around Lottie's waist.

Lottie thought she may have surprised the twins when she whispered, "I'm not," but the tear on her cheek betrayed the lie.

123

Chapter Seventeen

One Glimpse of Heaven

"Those men downstairs, who are they?"

Patrice washed her face and hands in the bowl on the dresser, while her maidservant stood by with a hand towel.

"Colonel Baker and some of my brother's friends."

"Those boys dressed like girls, the pretty ones, are they gal-boys?"

Patrice answered, "They are drummer boys, dressed as women for male entertainment. You'll find my brother and his friends have certain inclinations."

Lottie stood with her back to Patrice, looking out the front window of the second story bedroom once occupied by Aurora Cane, the matriarch of the Cane dynasty. She could see the other occupants of the room in their reflections on the window glass. Patrice pulled off the muslin cap that held her hair, letting her braid fall down her back.

She asked Lottie, "Does that concern you, these boys? I assure you none of them are here against their will."

"I know of men who make love with men. I'm not without some sophistication. I have read the Greeks."

"I was not implying—Thank you, Minnie. You can go."

"I put out the extra nightclothes like you asked, Miss Patrice." Minnie indicated Lottie. "Does the miss want help getting out of her garments?"

"Thank you, Minnie. I will help her."

"Well, okay. The water was real hot when I poured it in the bath. You might ought to wait a spell before getting in."

"Thank you, Minnie. I will be careful."

"Call me when you're ready to dump the water. I'll be up a spell."

"Thank you, Minnie. It'll be here in the morning. You can go on to sleep."

Lottie began to chuckle quietly. She watched the two women's reflections. Patrice stood in the open doorway in her untied corset and drawers trying to shut out her nosey old nanny.

"Do you want me to tell Herman to bring that supper up to you?"

"No, I couldn't eat a bite right now. Thank you." Patrice kissed the old woman's cheek. "Good night, Minnie."

Patrice pushed the door closed and turned the key in the lock.

"I can see that you are laughing."

"I think she is wary of your house guest," Lottie said, as she turned around to face her hostess.

Patrice sat on a chair to remove her bloodstained stockings, while she explained, "Minnie is quite protective of us. She was there the day we were born. Minnie's were the first hands to swaddle us and have been a source of comfort all our days."

"Is she free to go?"

Patrice put her stained stockings in a basket by the door, where Minnie had already placed the soiled apron, petticoat, skirt, and blouse. She came toward Lottie, which caused the latter's heart to flutter.

Patrice would answer Lottie's inquiry, but first, she asked a favor. She presented her back and asked, "Could you get that last button? I never can reach that one."

Lottie said, "Of course."

With five sisters, Lottie had aided in the dressing and undressing of females of all ages. Her fingers trembled on the button. She wondered why, while Patrice rattled on about Minnie and continued to disrobe.

"She is free. She could leave us."

Now in her natural state from the waist down, Patrice dropped the drawers Lottie helped unbutton in the basket by the door. They were made of fine white linen with fancy tucks and tatted trim around the bottoms. The only elegant undergarments Lottie had ever seen were on those French postcards she found in a knapsack discarded after the first battle of Goldsborough in '62. The ones she hid in the swamp because she couldn't bring herself to throw them away. Those postcards were the reason Lottie's hands trembled at the moment. The women on the cards were doing things with each other that Lottie had never imagined and then could not forget.

Patrice continued to speak as if nothing out of the ordinary was taking place. She unhooked the front of the corset Minnie had already loosened in the back.

"Grandmother provided for Minnie in her will, but all she has ever known is taking care of one Cane child after another."

Patrice stood facing Lottie with nothing on but a linen chemise. It was white with tucks of decorative needlework. Her nipples were clearly visible through the thin fabric. Lottie was sure Patrice must see the heat rising to her face. The glowing had begun in earnest.

"I love her as I would my own mother. She may stay as long as she likes. She nearly stayed in Philadelphia. Coming back to Wayne County wasn't in any of our plans."

When they arrived at Patrice and Patrick's home, Lottie had been rushed through to the upstairs, as the soldiers in the parlor were already into their cups. She had removed only her cape and hat. Patrice appeared ready to remedy that.

"Come, let's get you out of those clothes."

Lottie needed an excuse to leave. Conveniently, she had one at the ready. "Someone should go to Bullhead. Maybe there are wounded."

"If messages reached Patrick before the wounded reached the hospital, you can be assured someone other than Yankees was already at Bullhead."

"I haven't stepped foot on Edwards land since I was eleven years old," Lottie said, almost wistfully.

"We both have had complicated relationships with distant fathers, Lottie. Even so, I am so sorry you had to lose yours in this way."

"Maybe Calvin and the others are wrong. Maybe he's alive and hurt."

"Would you go to him, if you could? Has this changed the way you feel about Hub Edwards?" Patrice asked.

"How do you know how I feel about my father?"

Patrice's smile was disarming, appearing as if she knew things she couldn't. She said as much. "Bratcher Patch isn't the other end of the world. Everyone knows how you feel about the Edwards family. You never hid that."

Lottie looked out the window at the Yankees in the street and armed guards at every door. "I guess it does not matter how I feel. I can't get out of Goldsborough tonight." She turned back to Patrice. "I used to try to wash the Edwards off me after I misheard the adults saying I would never be clean of his mark."

"What did they mean? What mark?"

"I used to think there was a mark I couldn't see that told everyone I was illegitimate. Now, I think they were talking about the way I look. I'm told Jefferson and I look very much like young Hub."

Patrice shook her head. "If it were that easy to wash away family blemishes, I would have scrubbed myself raw by now. But alas, I'm stuck being the daughter of a man I despise."

Lottie smiled. "We do have a bit in common."

"Now, the sad part done with, let us have a night shut away from war and absent fathers. I'll happily share my bath with you. It would be a shame to let so much hot water go to one person." She moved toward Lottie again. "But first, we must remove all these clothes."

Lottie took a step back and bumped into the windowsill. She had nowhere to run. Patrice stopped moving. The two women stared at each other for what seemed to Lottie minutes but could have only been a few seconds. She watched Patrice's brow knit and then a slight smile of understanding crossed her lips.

"Is something wrong? Surely, with five sisters, you have been unclothed in sight of other women."

Before Lottie could stop the words, she said, "But they are sisters. You are—"

Patrice took another step closer. "I am, what? What is different about me from your sisters."

Lottie stood dumbfounded when Patrice moved even closer. She felt Patrice's breath on her cheek when the half-naked woman reached around to pull the heavy window curtains closed. Lottie was positive Patrice heard the sharp intake of breath her closeness had caused. The proof was in the grin she wore when she again looked into Lottie's eyes.

"Well, now. That answers that question."

Lottie found the words, though her closeness to Patrice made it difficult. "What question would that be?"

"I thought you might have a crush on my brother."

"And now?"

"And now, I think you might have other passions."

Lottie slid across the wall and away from Patrice, as she said, "I don't think I know what passion is."

Patrice did not advance quickly but remained in pursuit, or that is what it felt like to Lottie. As the fox hears the hounds and seeks its burrow, Lottie backpedaled across the room toward the door. It was then she saw the key had been removed and all hope of flinging the door open and running away was lost. Before she knew what was happening, Patrice was there, close, too close.

Lottie pressed her back against the door. Patrice, still wearing only the thin chemise, began to unbutton Lottie's blouse, one slow buttonhook at a time.

"Passion, Charlotte Bratcher, is that thumping in your heart just this second."

Lottie's blouse fell open. Patrice ran a finger along Lottie's jawline.

"It's the tightness in your chest, the feeling that you can't quite catch a full breath."

Patrice ripped the tails of Lottie's blouse from beneath the waist of her skirt roughly and then was suddenly gentle again as she slid the garment off her shoulders.

"Passion is the way you feel when I touch your skin, like fire and ice at the same time."

Patrice's fingertips turned Lottie's internal glowing to an eternal flame.

She brushed her lips across Lottie's. "Passion is when my lips touch yours and—"

Her mother and sisters told Lottie that girls often practiced kissing, in preparation for married lives. Now, seemed like as good a time as any to begin her lessons. Although Lottie had never kissed anyone passionately, it apparently came very naturally to her. She leaned closer, pressing her lips to Patrice's ever so lightly. With the first sparks of desire exploding inside her body, Lottie lost her reserve and pulled Patrice into her arms. The kiss deepened until she thought she might vanish there on that spot, consumed by the yearning for this woman.

Patrice moaned softly. Lottie had only imagined she had reached the climax of emotion until that soft sound reached her ear. Suddenly, Lottie couldn't breathe. She pushed Patrice off her chest and tore at the lacings on the working stays she wore instead of a corset.

At that moment, Lottie believed that she might die. Her chest heaved. Her heart raced. She perspired profusely. The heavy skirt and petticoat felt smothering. She tangled the laces of the confining garment, further complicating her predicament. Patrice seemed to realize what was happening.

"Hey, whoa, slow down. Come over here." Patrice led Lottie to the bed. "Sit down. Let me get you some water."

"Too hot." Lottie managed to say. "Help me out of these confinements."

It was no longer a passionate exercise. The two women flew at laces, buttons, and hooks that held Lottie captive until she stood in only the plain white muslin chemise passed down from an older sister and the drawers to match. Both undergarments were too small for the tallest of the Bratcher women but had served their purpose.

Lottie sat down on the edge of the bed, while Patrice fetched the water she had promised from a pitcher on the dresser. She returned and handed the glass to Lottie.

"I think I'll just let you cool off for a bit, while I bathe. I must wash all the hospital horror away," Patrice said, as she twisted the long braid of her hair into a pile on top of her head and pinned it there. "Are you feeling any better?"

"Some," was all Lottie had to say at the moment.

She still reeled from the kiss. Lottie drank the water while she chastised herself for nearly fainting. Passion, she surmised, was deadly. Out of the corner of her eye, Lottie saw the chemise lift over Patrice's head. This time, when the rush came, she met it with more resolve. In the seconds she had to decide not to look, she already had. Lottie slowed her breathing and watched Patrice Cole's body disappear into the copper tub of steaming water. The smell of roses filled the air.

"Lawd, have mercy," Lottie whispered.

Patrice didn't hear her. She rambled on about the bath as she washed. "I don't want Minnie to carry all this water up those stairs. I used to have the tub on the first floor, nearer to the kitchen, but when the Yankees came, she insisted we move it up here for privacy. I carry cold water up before I go to the hospital, so she only has to bring up the boiling water, and Herman hel—"

Before Patrice could finish her thought, Lottie asked, "Is this what you learned up north, how to seduce a woman?"

Patrice grinned through her reply, "Seduce a woman? Is that what I'm doing?"

Lottie smiled back. "Well, since I have never been kissed, or anything else, I'm merely guessing, but I think yes, you are."

"Never been kissed?" Patrice wore an expression of surprise.

"No, not once," Lottie answered.

"I suppose the boys were afraid to ask," Patrice said, with a sly grin.

"Well, I did hit Jacob Sumner with a riding crop when he tried a few years ago."

"I guess word got around," Patrice said, laughing.

Lottie laughed too. "I guess so."

The room grew quiet for a few seconds.

Patrice broke the silence with a question. "Should I be grateful there are no riding crops in this room?"

Lottie smiled at Patrice. She rose from the bed and crossed the room, where she placed the water glass on the dresser. Lottie then moved to the copper tub to stand over it. She unabashedly took in the splendor of a naked Patrice Cole.

Something changed in the room when Lottie removed her chemise and drawers. Patrice watched without saying a word. Lottie began to sense sexual power for the first time. She could see the want in the other woman's eyes and knew that the desires she felt were mutual.

"My God, but you are stunning," Patrice whispered.

"As are you," Lottie replied.

Patrice stood, held out her hand, and invited Lottie into the tub. Lottie stepped into the warm water, which only added to all the sensations she felt. There were so many, it threatened to overwhelm her again.

Patrice saw something in Lottie's expression that prompted her to say, "Breathe in through your nose, slowly."

Lottie did as she was told.

Patrice continued, "Now, out through your mouth. That's good."

"I feel too much," Lottie said when the world stopped spinning.

Patrice leaned in and brushed her lips against Lottie's, whispering, "This is only the beginning."

Lottie followed Patrice's direction down into the water. She sat facing her, pulling her knees up to allow Patrice space to kneel in front of her. The water rose to within inches of the top of the rolled edge. Lottie was afraid to move, for fear the water would escape, or worse, the tub was going to cave through the ceiling onto the gentlemen downstairs. Her fears became distant thoughts when Patrice lifted a tin cup of warm water and poured it slowly down Lottie's chest.

She started to speak, but Patrice put her index finger on Lottie's lips and said, "Shh."

Patrice dipped the cup and poured the water again, paying close attention to Lottie's nipples, which the latter did notice. Lottie felt the sensation go through her body. She felt the tension already building between her legs. Lottie's hands gripped the edge of the tub, as she slid down the slanted end. Her legs spread more and Patrice moved in to fill the void, while she continued to pour warm water over Lottie's body.

Lottie wanted to close her eyes and give into the pleasure, but was afraid to miss a moment of watching as Patrice began to bathe her with a sponge that smelled like roses.

She squirmed against Patrice's knee and once again tried to speak, "I don't kno—"

Patrice leaned forward, balancing herself with one hand on the edge of the tub, and kissed the words from Lottie's lips. She then moved down Lottie's neck, to her chest, and finally to a breast. Lottie pressed her chest up into Patrice's lips, arching her back with a moan that escaped her throat.

131

"Oh, God," she gasped when Patrice pressed in harder between Lottie's legs with one of her own.

Patrice dropped the sponge, pulled Lottie up out of the water and straddled one of her legs. Now, Lottie could feel the heat of Patrice's desires on her thigh, their wet bodies sliding together like a matching set. The sensation of her breasts against Patrice's caused Lottie to pull her lover closer with a need to meld with her, blend into one.

Patrice locked her fingers in Lottie's mass of curls and pulled her into a kiss. Their tongues found each other in a slow dance, the rhythm of which began to flow through them. Their bodies began to move together, slipping, sliding, pressing skin on skin. Lottie lost the sense of her surroundings. She knew nothing but Patrice—her hair, her smell, the feel of Patrice's skin against her fingertips. She'd never felt anything so soft, so smooth.

One of Patrice's hands left Lottie's hair and trailed down her cheek. The hand followed Lottie's neck down to a breast and squeezed the nipple, causing a shock wave and another gasp from Lottie. When Patrice's hand left Lottie's chest and began sliding further down her body, Lottie's breathing became short and quickened with each inch lower it traveled. When Patrice reached the inside of Lottie's thigh, her other hand dropped from Lottie's hair to the small of her back and drew her in close.

Patrice pulled her lips from Lottie's and looked deep into her eyes. She slipped her hand between Lottie's legs and whispered, "Remember to breathe."

Chapter Eighteen

Familial Relations
March 26, 1865

In the hazy sleep just before wakefulness, Lottie heard "Reveille" trumpet through Goldsborough. Moments later the morning gun fired, and the sounds of a besieged city coming to life crept into her dreams come true.

"Can we stay this way forever?" Patrice whispered, pressing her back into Lottie's body.

Lottie tightened her arms around Patrice, burying her nose in that coal-black hair. She smelled the rose water and took a deep breath, inhaling Patrice, holding her fragrance inside, before letting it slowly float away.

"I will never forget last evening, nor the way we fit so perfectly together," she whispered into Patrice's ear, before kissing a little patch of neck exposed between long strands of hair. "It's as if we are a matching pair."

Patrice turned in Lottie's arms to face her. "I will never let you forget, Charlotte Bratcher. I would wake with you the rest of my life, if it were up to me."

Lottie leaned in to Patrice's lips—

The intimacy ended abruptly when the bedroom door burst open. The reminder of another existence outside the walls came in the form of Patrice's twin, already dressed and looking dashing.

"Good morning, sister," Patrick said, as he entered the room with a silver service of coffee and biscuits. He looked around at the various items of clothing spread about the room and using the toe of his boot shut the bedroom door behind him. "I thought I'd save you the dressing down Minnie would give you if she saw this debauchery."

Lottie rolled away from Patrice, threw the duvet over her head, and hid.

Patrick placed the tray on the bedside table. "Too late. I'm aware of your presence, Miss Bratcher, and your scandalous behavior with my wayward sister."

Lottie poked her head out from under the cover. "How do you know that?" She looked at Patrice for a clue.

"He didn't, but he does now."

"Oh," Lottie said and pulled the duvet tightly up to her chin.

"Women are so peculiar about modesty and sex," Patrick noted, as he threw open the heavy curtain, letting in the dawn.

"Only because men have made it necessary to conceal our bodies from their primal lust," Patrice countered.

"I have no such yearnings for female flesh," Patrick said, with a wink to his sister. "You may expose yourself, Miss Bratcher. I assure you it will not induce animalistic behavior."

Lottie gripped the covers tightly and replied, "Delphia Lane might be surprised to know that. I think she has other plans for you."

"I have no intention of marrying Miss Lane, but we shall keep that our secret for the time being. Jack arranged this affair for his own profit. He arranged one for Patrice, as well."

Her expression must have shown that Lottie had no knowledge of this arranged marriage.

Patrick responded, "Sister, you didn't tell your guest that you are to be married to her half-brother. I suppose we'll have to wait to see what the Yankees do to him after last night's escapade."

The duvet fell away, as Lottie forgot she was naked and sat up. "Calvin? You are engaged to marry Calvin Edwards?"

"My goodness, Miss Bratcher. I had no idea that under your customary male attire lay such a stunning specimen of womanhood. Maybe I will change my proclivities, just this once."

Patrick began to remove his vest.

Lottie hurriedly covered her breasts.

"Patrick, stop teasing her and hand me my dressing robe."

"As you wish, dear sister. Although, it would only be fair to share."

Patrick re-buttoned his vest and grabbed the robe from the chair where Patrice had tossed it after a late night visit to the pantry for sustenance. Patrice climbed out of bed, completely at ease with her nakedness in front of her brother. She slipped on the robe and then placed her hands on Patrick's chest and pushed him toward the door.

"There are things, dear brother, that we do not share. Lottie is one of them. Thank you for the coffee. Now, be gone."

Patrick backed toward the door, saying, "I brought her things out of the wagon."

He reached outside the door, producing Lottie's satchel, which contained her trousers, hat, pistol, and boots. She had intended to wear the women's clothes while depositing Harper at the hospital and then change into riding attire for the trip home.

Patrice pushed her brother out the door. "Thank you. Now, go."

Lottie was already on her feet by the time the door closed. It was evident to Patrice that her new lover was upset because she immediately started explaining.

"Lottie, I have no intention of ever marrying Calvin Edwards. The Coles and the Edwards made a land deal with me as the price. I won't be exchanged like chattel."

Patrice placed Lottie's satchel on the bed.

Lottie reached for it while asking, "Does Calvin know about this arrangement?"

"I have no idea. Patrick overheard a conversation between Harriet and Jack, making wedding plans. Delphia is Harriet's cousin, so it's Lane land in the deal too. I was never consulted."

"I'd rather not have anything else in common with Calvin Edwards," Lottie said curtly, as she opened the satchel and took out the pistol, which she placed on the bed.

"You can't honestly believe I would consent to marry that toad."

Lottie snapped back, "As if you will have a choice in what you do. Jack will have his way. He'll not let that Cane fortune go too far,

135

and he'll get a fair piece of land in the deal. I'd be careful. Rumor has it Canes don't live long around Jack Cole."

"A fact I'm well aware of. He gets nothing no matter where or with whom I live my life. Jack can never have a penny of Cane money. It's in Grandmother's will."

"So, he sells you to the highest bidder for his profit. If you believe he had something to do with your mother's death, what makes you think you can defy him without consequence? I understand she tried."

Lottie pulled on the drawers she had dropped the night before and then dumped the remaining contents of the satchel on the floor.

"Why are you so fixated on my marriage prospects today, when they were of no concern to you last night?" Patrice demanded.

Lottie picked up the trousers first and slipped them on.

"Lottie, stop dressing and look at me," Patrice implored.

Reluctantly, Lottie raised her eyes to meet Patrice's and spoke, "I have enjoyed your company, Miss Cole, but I need to go home. Although I despised my father, other members of my family did not. I should be with them."

"You still need the pass to get through the pickets. I will come with you."

Lottie found her blouse on the floor, where it had been tossed, along with her chemise and working stays. Her skirt and petticoat she gathered from the chaise lounge by the window.

While she claimed her possessions, she asked, "What makes it so easy for you and your brother to pass through the pickets? Are you Union spies?"

"Why are you acting like this?"

Lottie didn't answer. She pulled the chemise over her head and shoved her arms into the blouse. Everything else went into the satchel.

Patrice continued her entreaties. "An hour ago you were kissing me, and now you act as if you can't bear the sight of me."

Lottie struggled with buttoning her blouse. Patrice took a few steps closer but did not offer to help.

"Last night, you said you didn't know what passion was. I suspect you do now. Can you leave me, Lottie? Can you keep yourself from loving me?"

Lottie stopped dressing, tears welling in her eyes. "I can't love you, Patrice. I'd rather not endure the eventuality of your marriage to any man, even if it isn't my half-brother."

"What if you marry first? Whose heart will be broken then?"

"Ha! I'll never marry a man. No man is ever going to have his way with me. And I will not be your secret lover. I will not be what my mother was to anyone, man or woman. I will not love something I cannot keep for my own."

"Well, then I will not marry either. We will collect my share of the estate funds when the time comes and live up north. We'll tell everyone we're spinster sisters or cousins. I think cousins since we look nothing alike."

"Patrice, it is your wealth that ultimately divides us."

Patrice smiled, a sweet turn of the corner of her lips that challenged Lottie's resolve to be done with this—this, whatever this was. Everything was so new it had not yet been given a formal address in Lottie's mind. She wanted to stay in bed with the heat of this woman against her skin. She wanted Patrice's fingers tangled in her hair again, their lips pressed together, tongues entwined. Lottie wanted so much she knew she would never have, never again, not after today. It, this thing with no name, could never be.

"I would live poor with you, Lottie, but why, if we don't have to? We can travel the world, you and I. We never have to set foot in Wayne County again."

Lottie continued buttoning her blouse, focusing on the task instead of Patrice's eyes.

"One night of lovemaking may rid you of all familial responsibilities, Patrice, but not I. It is exactly because you can leave Wayne County without a second thought that we cannot see each other again. I have a brother with one leg, a brother-in-law who seems done for, another who is missing, and Jefferson doesn't live in Bratcher Patch anymore. He'll have his own land now that Pa's dead. Hub did right by his sons. He left his daughters and his concubine for me to tend to, it seems."

Lottie tucked the tails of the blouse and the chemise into the trousers and buttoned the front flap. She added a belt over the flap to keep the trousers up. They were Jefferson's and slightly too large to stay up on their own. Besides, Lottie needed a way to carry the ever-present pistol that gave her much of the swagger she possessed. Without it, she was an unarmed, unescorted female. In the world Lottie lived in, that was one of the worst things she could be. She sat down on the edge of the bed to pull on her stockings and boots.

Patrice came to sit beside her. "Then, I will stay here with you," she said, as if such a thing could be done.

Lottie turned her head to look at Patrice and immediately regretted the choice, but she said, "If you stay here, Jack will marry you off to someone. A woman like you will not stay unwed long."

"Marriages are contracts. They speak nothing of love," Patrice challenged. "And what do you mean, a woman like me?"

"Patrice, you are elegant and educated, the perfect mate for the landed gentry, not to mention the dowry that accompanies you."

"I'm not horseflesh to be bred to the stud who pays for the privilege with a plot of land Jack has been coveting."

"You are able to make that pronouncement only because you can afford to leave." Lottie stood up into the last boot, snapping her heel down hard. She stuck the pistol under the belt at the back of her trousers. "If you stay, you'll be married soon enough, at whatever price Jack sets. That is the world we live in, Patrice, a man's world."

"And yet you state emphatically that you will never marry. How is it that you are granted special dispensation?"

Lottie stood in front of Patrice, looking down at her. "Because men aren't looking for poor girls to marry. There are far more of us than your kind. They'll get to the willing types before they come knocking on my door out in Bratcher Patch. In fact, I've been assured by Jane that no man will ever have me."

Patrice looked up at Lottie. "She's wrong. Those men's clothes don't hide your beauty. I find it rather attractive. I think that was when I knew I loved you. I came home the first time, after being gone for nearly a year. When I stepped down from the train, you were there, waiting for someone else. The sun framed you perfectly, there in your long-coat straddling Big John, your hair hanging in ringlets under the brim of your hat. You were Joan of Arc on a steed, magnificent."

Lottie felt the heat from Patrice's words. She was hypnotizing, intoxicating, a siren luring her prey onto the rocks. Lottie took a step back, resolute in her decision to never touch Patrice Cole again. She could not and be expected to ever let her go.

As she reached down to the floor for her satchel and hat, Lottie asked a question to stop her heart listening to the siren's song. "Where is this plot of land Delphia offered so Calvin could take your hand?"

It was Patrice who looked away this time. Lottie became alarmed unexpectedly, and for a good reason, it would seem.

"Patrice, where is this land?"

"Lottie, I'm sorry."

"What? What are you saying?"

"Hubbard Edwards owns Bratcher Patch. Your mother couldn't pay the taxes. Jack was going to get that land one way or another, so Hub paid the taxes in exchange for a piece of the land. By January this year, he had most of it back in the Edwards' estate."

Lottie lashed out. "That's not true. Jane paid the taxes from money John Simpson had put up."

"Jane lied to you. She knew what you would say."

Lottie crossed the room in a flash and grabbed the black cloak from where it hung on the back of the door. She put on the hat and cape and turned back to Patrice.

"How do you know so much about things you shouldn't? You and your brother seem to be very much aware of the comings and goings out at Bratcher Patch. What are you playing at, Patrice Cole?"

Patrice stood and turned to face Lottie, her robe falling open. Lottie assumed that was a planned attempt to keep her there, which might have worked if she hadn't been so damned mad. She ducked her chin, tipping the brim of her hat, picked up the satchel, and then opened the door to leave.

From behind, she heard Patrice say, "Charlotte Bratcher, are you going to break my heart?"

Patrice's answer came in the echo of boot steps walking away.

Chapter Nineteen

Hell Before Breakfast

"Mr. Cole, would you tell me where I might find my wagon and horse?"

Patrick sat on the ornately milled porch railing with his back leaned against a turned porch column, watching people pass on the street. The Cane residence was among the newer homes in Goldsborough; an example of modern excess with its steeply pitched gable roof and decorative glass.

"Hum, that was a quick exit. You didn't even take time for coffee. Only my dear sister could make someone angry enough to walk away from real coffee in these thin times."

"My horse?"

"I see the romance has soured. That was a whirlwind, wasn't it?"

Lottie scowled at him.

"Around back in the stable. Your mare was fed and watered this morning with the others."

"Thank you. I appreciate your hospitality." Lottie stepped down from the porch before she turned back to ask, "Patrick, did you give a note to John Simpson? Are you watching me?"

"No, dear, I assure you, I am not watching you. I may have been out your way a time or two, but it isn't you I'm concerned with. My sister, however, has been focused on you for years."

"It'll come to nothing. Why even begin?" Lottie replied.

"I think the beginning already happened," Patrick said with a chuckle. "I suspect it isn't over yet, either."

"Why do you say that?"

"Because I know my sister."

"Yes, but you don't know me. Once I've made up my mind to leave it, it gets left. Ask my father."

Patrick grimaced. "Ooh, now that's a bit awkward."

"That's another thing. How do you know my father is really dead? Who told you what happened out there?"

Patrick dropped the devil may care attitude he usually displayed for everyone. He stepped down into the yard with Lottie and leaned in very close. With the cape covering Lottie's attire, but not her curls, to passersby, they appeared as lovers saying early morning goodbyes.

"Lottie, you will get us all killed if you keep asking questions. Just like no one needs to know what you have stashed in the swamp. Let it be. It will all be over soon enough."

Before Lottie could react to Patrick's knowledge of the men hiding in Appletree Swamp, a carriage drove by slowly. It carried one of the young debutantes from the town and her old grandmother, driven by their manservant. If there were not blue coats stirring in the dawn's early light, it could have been business as usual on a Sunday morning in Goldsborough.

The young woman called out, "Lottie Bratcher seen leaving Patrick Cole's residence at the crack of dawn, unescorted. My, what will Delphia Lane have to say about her fiancé caught with such trash? Taking up your mother's profession, Lottie?"

Patrick looked over his shoulder at the passing carriage and then back to Lottie. He said softly, "My apologies for this forwardness, but it is in both our best interests, as you will soon discover."

Without another word, and before rage caused Lottie to charge into the street after the arrogant debutante, Patrick enfolded her into his arms and kissed her. Caught off guard, Lottie pressed her hands against his chest. He felt different from his sister, hard-muscled with facial hair that bristled against her skin. No, Lottie didn't like kissing a man at all. Before her resistance could become too adamant for the ruse to play for its audience, Patrick rereleased her.

The ladies in the carriage were sufficiently scandalized.

"Give the whip to the horse, Alfred," the offended young woman said. "And be quick about it."

Patrick chuckled, saying, "Well, now, Sunday dinner gossip should be all a tither with the news of our scandalous affair."

"I imagine the preacher's two boys being dead will be foremost in the congregation's minds."

Patrick showed a rare flash of temper. "That fool Jack and his greed got those boys killed."

Lottie pointed out. "When Jack finds out he'll not profit off your nuptials, he'll come for you, Patrick. If he can't get to you, he'll get to Patrice. I don't think her fiancé is going to be around much longer either if he isn't dead already."

"I'm afraid Calvin has left us. I was informed of his passing early this morning, but didn't think you would care," Patrick said.

"I don't," Lottie replied. "Does anyone know where Harriet was during the attack? She's the only one left if she's still alive."

"I wouldn't doubt that she is with Jack somewhere, Lottie. There is a lot you do not know about the goings on at Bullhead."

"As I'm learning," Lottie said. "You watch out for Jack, and I'll worry about Harriet Lane Edwards."

Patrick added, "Jack has more pressing problems than to whom I am married. When the Yankees find him, he'll pay for what happened last night. He's probably still looking for Gabriel. The little weasel is doubtless in Virginia by now."

"How do the Yankees know it was Jack out at Bullhead? Did you tell them?"

"Shall I kiss you again to stop your inquisition?"

"No, that will not be necessary," Lottie said as she backed away.

"There are forces at work here that have your best interests at heart, even if they can't tell you what they are up to."

"I've had enough of secrets and secret lives, Patrick. I am going now. I'll take the saddle and leave the buckboard here. I can travel faster without it."

"You still need a travel pass," Patrick said.

"Dr. Davis said I just needed to ask the Provost Marshall. Do you know where he can be found?"

"Conveniently, the Provost set up an office in Dr. Davis's house."

"Well, Doc isn't there anyway. He and Mary have been living at the hospital for over a year now." Lottie began to walk away. "Thank you for the hospitality, Mr. Cole. I'll be going, now."

"Is there anything I should tell my sister," he asked.

"I believe I left it where it should stand," Lottie said, but did not know if she really meant it.

Patrick smiled at her. "Don't slam the door too hard, Charlotte. It is a rare love she has for you. She'll not give up."

Lottie turned away.

"Lottie," Patrick called and waited for her full attention. "Tiller is still out there. Be careful."

"Goodbye, Patrick. Whatever it is you two are up to, I hope it doesn't get you killed."

Lottie saddled the mare and rode over to Dr. Davis's home. She was careful not to look back at the Cole house; chiefly avoiding the upstairs windows where she knew Patrice was watching her. Lottie learned what passion, lust, love, and leaving felt like in less than twelve hours. Crying wasn't an option, so she swallowed all of it and concentrated on what she had to do next.

In many ways, the poor fared better than the rich after four years of war. At least out in Bratcher Patch, where Lottie's family had always made do with what they had, things were not as desperate as they were for those who had the necessities of life perpetually provided for them. A man, who paid taxes on a million dollars worth of property before the war, now stood in line at the Provost Marshal's office to draw rations from the Union army. The line stretched out the door, even on this Sunday morning. Lottie recognized half the wealthiest people in town waiting for the necessary papers to feed on the teat of the very Union they forced people like Lottie's brothers to fight.

Lottie dared not dismount, for fear of losing the mare to a thief. If she waited in line, it would be hours before the Provost Marshall would see her. Lottie rode toward Center Street, while she weighed her chances of escaping town without a pass and without getting shot.

On every corner, soldiers congregated trading watches, rings, and jewelry of all descriptions. Some had pieces of silver cut out of solid serving dishes, revolvers, gold pieces, all prizes from the march to the sea were up for sale to the highest bidder. Between the buildings on Center Street, down the alleys, groups crowded together to wager on games of chance. Poker games played out right on the sidewalk for a dollar a game.

"Hey, will you trade horses," says one mounted fella to another.

"What would you give me?"

"Well, yours didn't cost nothing, and neither did mine, so that's an even trade."

Lottie watched the men switch horses. She pulled the brim down on her hat and headed for the center of town. The Borden Hotel sat back from the street about sixty feet in an elm grove. Across from it were the repaired but still charred remains of the railroad platform and a train making steam.

"Do something about those damned dead animals. Get those half-dead ones rounded up and out of town. Get control of those bummers before I return. I gave an order for restraint. By God, I will have it."

Lottie remained on horseback on the west side of Center Street observing General William Tecumseh Sherman walk to the train. Freckled and redheaded with a gray-speckled beard, Lottie marveled at how unlike the fiend she had imagined while reading newspaper accounts of his march to the sea he seemed.

"How'd this Reb manage to keep a well-fed thoroughbred?"

Lottie felt the man next to her step closer. She looked down to see one of the men she recognized from Tiller's gang. He realized he knew her too.

"You! Hey, it's that girl!"

The man reached for the reins of the mare. Had Lottie been on Big John, this would have been when he stepped in to save his girl. The mare, however, spooked at having her head jerked to the side. When she whinnied nervously and let loose with a loud burst of flatulence, it scared the mare, causing her to rear up and paw the air with her front hoofs.

She was young and flighty, in need of training, and probably off the farm for the first time. Some of Hubbard Edwards's stock got skittishness with the speed he bred into them. It was Uncle William's horse, but Lottie recognized the telltale blaze on the mare's forehead upon first sight. The dam that originated that white splash would crash through a fence if spooked. She was fast, but she was crazy. Lottie had her hands full in an instant.

"Whoa, girl," Lottie said, as the mare lost her mind.

Lottie balanced in the saddle and squeezed her knees into the mare's ribs. She gave her a gentle kick with both heels.

"A horse can't rear when it's moving," Hub had told her.

When the mare's front hoofs hit the ground, Lottie reined her head into her right shoulder, driving her into a spin that cleared some space for them both, and then brought the horse under control. Her wild eyes and snorts warned of a future loss of composure, but for the moment, the mare stood perfectly still, as did everyone near the platform.

"Why isn't this fellow in my Cavalry? That was an amazing display of horsemanship. Who are you, sir?"

Lottie looked over at the railroad platform, where Sherman had apparently watched the entire episode.

The man that had grabbed the reins shouted, "That ain't no fella. That there is a woman and she killed two of Tiller's men."

Sherman stepped down from the platform and walked straight to the mare's nose, where he quieted her with clucks and whispers. Lottie made eye contact with him, the man of so much lore. What was genuine and what wasn't did not matter at the moment. The mare recognized the stallion in the herd. She calmed as he cooed to her. This was a horseman.

"This girl here killed two men, is that so?" Sherman asked Tiller's man.

The man at Lottie's left took off his hat and dipped his head in reverence while answering, "Yes, sir, General. She got this horse that Tiller wants. It ain't this one, but another. Billy and Miles went to get it and ain't been seen since."

"I'm not concerned with two of Tiller's bootlickers gone missing." Lottie spread her arms. "Look around. There is a war on. Men disappear every day. My father was killed last night. We're all just trying to survive this madness."

The words were out of her mouth before she knew she was going to say them.

"You have my condolences, Miss—I'm sorry, I don't know your name."

"Charlotte, sir, but they call me Lottie. Lottie Bratcher."

"Did your father teach you to handle a horse like that?" Sherman asked.

Lottie had to admit it. "Yes, sir. He did."

"What's so special about this horse you say this Tiller wants, Miss Charlotte Bratcher?"

"His name is Big John. He is my brother. Surely, a horseman like you understands that. He is big. He is fast. And would die fighting to his last breath before he would let a man sit on his back that he didn't want there."

Tiller's man interrupted. "She rides that animal like a tornader, General. It's a sight to behold."

"They would end up killing him because he will never bow to them, never break. He's my horse. Big John knows that and that I would die for him."

"I do understand the love of a good horse. Have you seen these missing men?"

Lottie didn't lie. She merely bent the truth of what she knew. "No, sir. I did not see those men. What I have seen is this man and those three over there roaming Wayne County stealing horses from poor folks and armies alike and selling to both sides, profiteering on the plight of others. Tiller ships the best ones up north to sell. They're thieves, plain and simple, with allegiance to none."

Sherman said nothing. He just nodded at another man in officer's attire. Lottie didn't know ranking but surmised the fella was pretty high up in the hierarchy by the way a group of soldiers responded to his order.

"Take these four into custody."

A commotion began as the men were detained and moved off to the makeshift prison on the edge of town. Their fate was of no concern to Lottie. At least they wouldn't be following her home.

Sherman ignored the scuffle at his back and patted the mare's neck. He said to Lottie, "The South is going to need women like you, Miss Bratcher. I go now to meet with President Lincoln in City Point and General Grant. Is there a message I can send them from you."

Lottie glanced around at the ragged soldiers and people, haggard from war, having forgotten long ago why they fought in the first place.

"Keep in mind that most of us were not consulted about this secession," Lottie said. "The worst has already been done to the working folks that will ultimately pay for the South's redemption."

146

"You're a bright young woman, Miss Bratcher. I will pass on your sentiments to Mr. Lincoln. Now, is there anything else I can do for you before I go?"

"I delivered a sick man to the hospital to have his leg cut off. I need a pass out to go home."

Sherman nodded to another soldier, who pulled a pre-printed form from a leather binder and stepped closer to Lottie. He produced a pencil from his pocket and jotted the place and date on the line at the top, under the words "Office of the Provost Marshall General."

"Full name, Miss Bratcher," he said.

Sherman stroked the mare's shoulder while Lottie answered, "Charlotte Bratcher."

"Going to?" The pencil-wielding soldier asked next.

"Home."

"I understand that, but where is home?"

"Bratcher Patch."

"Is that an actual place?"

A chuckle rippled through the crowd.

Sherman interrupted the inquiry. "Give her free rein. She'll not be a problem."

"Yes, sir," the soldier replied and filled in the remainder of the travel pass with no further input from Lottie.

Sherman spoke to Lottie again, "You'll be careful on your journey? Do you wish an escort?"

"No, sir. I can move faster on my own."

"I imagine that to be true," Sherman replied, showing a slight grin to Lottie as he nodded his head. "This is fine horse. Is she yours?"

"My uncle's, sir."

"She's young, but she is a fine thoroughbred. Wade Hampton would be jealous."

"My father thinks so, or thought so, as it were."

"Your father bred this horse?"

"Yes, sir."

"The horse world lost a good man then."

The General's scribe handed the pass to Lottie. It allowed her free movement within Wayne County.

"Thank you, General, on both counts."

"I should like to meet this Big John, Miss Bratcher. You will bring him to see me when I return."

"Yes, sir."

"Then I bid you good morning."

Sherman walked to the platform. Just before he stepped onto the train, he turned to the soldiers and citizens who gathered to get a glimpse of the great man himself—Ol' Cump, Uncle Billy.

"Let it be known, I'll have no lawless thieving. Rein it in boys, or I'll be forced to do it for you. These four will be dealt with severely before sunset today. Let it be a warning. Rein it in boys."

Sherman entered the train car, followed by a small group of men. Another man took his place on the platform. Lottie recognized him from the hospital. It was the angry captain.

"And hear me, now. I will also not stand for these home patrols challenging my men. I strung one of you bastards up and sent him to hell before breakfast. I'll do the same to all I catch. Like the General said, rein it in boys, or I will do it for you." The captain locked his gaze on Lottie. Even without the dress, he recognized her. He aimed his next comment straight at her, "If you know the scoundrel's family, they can cut him down on the way out of town, just beyond the last picket. You've been warned."

Chapter Twenty

Have Mercy

Loblolly is said to be a Native American name for low, wet area. That is where the loblolly pine is found growing in the maritime forests and coastal plain of North Carolina, near swamps and bodies of water. For five miles out from the center of Goldsborough, not a single mature tree remained standing as far as Lottie could see. Not a longleaf pine, not a pond pine, and not a single elm or oak of any size, not one of the trees that crowded in thick around every plowed field and wetland had been spared until she reached the giant loblolly at the fork in the road.

Taking the left fork, Lottie would continue on toward Faro and home. If she chose the right fork, Lottie would cross southeast to Thompson's farm and join up with the easterly running Bullhead Road. But currently, she sat on the mare, staring up at the first grown tree that she had seen since leaving town. It was an ancient loblolly pine, sturdily maintaining this post for decades, as evidenced by its massive trunk and thick branches. One of those resolute limbs reached out over the road, jutting about ten feet off the ground, and from it Calvin Edwards hung by the neck.

"I don't believe I've ever seen me no lynched white boy. I seen plenty o' colored folk strung up, but this here is a first."

"They hung thirteen white boys at once down in Kinston last February. Said they deserted the state and joined the blue coats.

Still, like you say, I ain't never seen a white boy just strung up in a tree out here on the road. He done somethin' awful, to be sure."

"What ya' reckon that sign there say?"

"It says, 'Civilian patrols be warned,'" Lottie read to the two old men.

They looked up at Lottie, who was still seated in the saddle. Neither had a full set of teeth and offered scraggly smiles, as they doffed their hats to her. Both parties took a minute to decide if this meeting would be a pleasant one. The two men knew it wasn't the place of a colored man to speak to an unaccompanied white female. They waited, hats in hand, eyes now on the ground.

"Pick your head up. You owe me no reverence," Lottie said.

Visibly relieved, one of the men said, "I guess them Yankees is takin' no prisoners. Not makin' light of this poor boy's lynchin', miss."

"Help me cut 'em down," Lottie said, as she slid off the horse's back.

"Naw, ma'am. Them Yankees will kill us for sure. What they hung up there needs to be left alone," the shorter of the two said.

"Family can cut him down. The man that strung him up there said so," Lottie answered.

"Is you family?"

"He's my father's son. Help me put him on my horse."

The two men exchanged looks and shrugs, before following Lottie to the base of the tree.

The short one asked, "Don't mean to be askin' what I don't need to know, but if he your father's son, ain't he your brother?"

Lottie shook her head, as she maneuvered the mare over by the tree and out of the way. She made sure to tie the skittish animal securely. "No. We share only the man that lay with our mothers. Nothing more."

The taller one chuckled. "Works that way down in the quarters sometime too."

"You got somethin' we can lay him on? 'Cause he surely foul. They bowels leave 'em when the rope get tight."

Lottie pulled a stag knife from her saddlebag and started for the tree. "Pull that rolled up gum blanket off the back of my saddle. We'll bind him in that."

The Yankees had thrown a rope over the branch and then strung Calvin up above the road. They tied off the other end around the tree trunk. Lottie chopped at the line with one sharp blow from the knife. Calvin's body plummeted with a thump to the hard-packed road.

"Glad they tied that corn bag 'roun' his head. That's always the worst part, seein' that tongue all black and swollen, eyes poppin' out they head."

"Don't 'magine she wants the details, Elbert."

"Uh, yeah, sorry, miss."

"I'm taking him to his mother. Calvin Edwards was a brutal boy and becoming a malevolent man. I don't much care how he faired."

Lottie did not need to share with these men that she had some business with the dead man's mother, Harriet Lane Edwards, the only living person standing between Lottie and the deed to Bratcher Patch. This bit of civil war had been brewing since the day Charlotte Bratcher was born. Joan of Arc, she wasn't, but Lottie was an angry young woman with her own brand of righteous vengeance driving her to battle.

Lottie walked over to Calvin's body. He'd been stripped down to his bloodstained, ordure-soiled long johns and had a burlap sack pulled over his head, synched tight by a hangman's noose.

"You want us to get that rope from 'round his neck 'fore we roll him up in here?"

"No, leave it. His mother should see what became of her boy, what evil she spawned on the world."

The two men stopped and stared at Lottie, seemingly unsure of who the evil one really was in this picture.

Lottie gave them a wry smile. "If it were me strung up in that tree, he would have left me for the buzzards. I won't leave him to that fate, but I don't have to give a damn that he's gone."

That satisfied the men. The taller one studied Calvin and then looked over at the mare.

"This big boy here and you ain't going far on that little filly. We can make a pole-frame sled with some of this rope," he paused to smile at Lottie, "leavin' the noose where it is, but cuttin' some off. Then you can pull him, and it won't tax your horse none."

Lottie looked around. "We're a bit short on poles for a frame."

151

"There's bamboo down at the bottom of that bank yonder, already cut down. Yankees didn't take it when they took the rest."

"Well, that was nice of them to leave that for us," Lottie said with a chuckle that made them all laugh.

They set about the task at hand and within fifteen minutes had a travois attached to the saddle, with Calvin's shrouded body tied to the two long poles joined by a rope-framed sled.

Back in the saddle, Lottie thanked the two men, "I really appreciate your help. I wish I could do more than thank you. If you're hell-bent on going to Goldsborough, then I can offer you this. Go to the girls' seminary. It's a hospital now. Ask for Dr. Davis. Tell him Lottie sent you. Tell the pickets you are going to work at the hospital. You'll at least get fed."

"Thank you very much, Miss Lottie. You be careful now."

"You keep that knife handy and your pistol dry," the other said. "Bad folks is everywhere."

Lottie clucked to the mare and waved her hat to the two men. Down the old path toward Bullhead she went, with the pole-frame sled bouncing along behind. Much had changed since the last time she set foot on Hub Edwards's property. More had changed since yesterday. Lottie had experienced ecstasy and agony in less than one trip of the earth around the sun. She had the rest of the two and a half hours to Bullhead to think on it.

The first and shortest leg of the journey took her along an old farm path. The saplings along the road had been left alone when the rest of the land was stripped. It offered a bit of cover, but Lottie stayed alert, her eyes continually searching her surroundings. She glanced back down the path, from where she came, making sure she wasn't followed. Her eyes fell on Calvin's trussed up body.

"Well now, Calvin. It looks like I bested you in the end." A grin crept across her face. She whispered over her shoulder, "I had my way with your betrothed. I suppose I won that round too."

Lottie pulled the cape closer against the biting wind. Her oil coat would have been better versus March's waning howls. The mare moved along at a four-beat walk, and Lottie's mind began to wander—not so much wander, as focus upon the moment Patrice gave herself over to her. In a flash, she was there—Patrice's breathing coming short and fast against her neck, then the gasp and shudder. Lottie swallowed hard, her pulse quickened, while her body relived the moment. She adjusted her seat in the saddle, but could not break the spell of that memory.

Everything around her disappeared as her mind raced back to the bed where she kissed Patrice for hours, explored every inch of her body, and learned what ecstasy truly was. Arms and legs entwined, desperately out of breath at times, then breathing each other in, melding together through long slow kisses, and deepening to desperation again. What she experienced making love with Patrice was more than Lottie had fantasized because she lacked the knowledge to imagine all that it could be.

It was as if they both knew that one night would be all they ever had, and it was over. All Lottie was ever going to know of love would be those memories. Forgetting Patrice Cole would never happen, but leaving her alone had to. Lottie was not the type to conform to social conventions out of fear of stigma. Still, even she knew loving Patrice Cole would come to no good. The old biddies ran about discussing Lottie's attire and how she rode a horse astride and handled a horse like a man.

"Imagine what they would think of how I handled Patrice," Lottie said, as she chuckled to herself.

The mare's ears perked up as the noise of traffic on the main road reached her. They had traveled alone for the thirty-minute trip on the crossroad, with Lottie lost in rose water fantasies and the scent of a woman. They would now join the northeastern artery into and out of Goldsborough, Bullhead Road. Just as the road came into view, Lottie heard a familiar voice.

"Well, well, I'm going to owe my sister a purse or gold," Patrick said. "She was sure you would fetch that wretched man and take him to his mother. I said you were cold-hearted and would let him swing. My apologies for the way I misjudged you, Miss Bratcher."

Patrick Cole stepped out of the tree cover running near a branch of Stoney Creek where he watered his mount. There next to his chestnut bay stood its twin and Patrick's. Patrice stepped toward the path, where Lottie brought the mare to a halt.

"I couldn't let you do this alone, Lottie. We're coming with you, and that is that."

Patrick grinned at Lottie. "See, I told you."

He stepped over to Patrice's horse and made a hand-step for his sister, who used it to climb onto her sidesaddle. She wore a stylish, indigo, velveteen riding habit, a cavalier style hat with chinstrap, ribbon, and feather to match. Her coal-black hair fell over her shoulders down to her horse's hindquarters. Patrice Cole was a vision.

The "have mercy" of Lottie's thoughts remained unsaid, but Patrick saw it in her face, according to his comment.

"She does have that effect on people. Stunning, isn't she?"

"My grandmother spent an enormous amount of money on clothing. Half of which she never wore. Luckily, I have grown into her most recent purchases, a bit outdated now, but new."

The old Lottie woke to rebuild the walls. "Heaven forbid you must wear 1850s fashion."

"Lottie, I'm not going to play that game with you anymore. You like me. You can't help it. Now, hush and let's deliver this man to his mother and be done with the deed."

Lottie sat up a little taller in the saddle, her shock evidently showing.

Patrick mounted his horse and let out a full-throated laugh, before he said, "Give up, Lottie. The ball has begun, you might as well dance."

Patrick moved out in front of Lottie to clear their way into the slow-moving traffic on Bullhead Road. The scent of roses reached Lottie as Patrice rode up beside her. Miss Cole had made up her mind about how things were going to be. Lottie had no choice in the matter.

Chapter Twenty-One

Sins of the Father

The home where Hubbard Edwards had been born stood a few hundred yards from the main house, down the well-worn path to the abandoned servants' quarters. Lottie's brothers, James and Jefferson, had been born in the "quarter" too. The cabin in which they drew their first breaths remained standing as well. The stables were intact, the barns uninjured, the fences stood guarding empty pastures. However, all that remained of the turn of the century plantation manor in which Lottie's grandfather Brantley Edwards had the good fortune to have been born were two pairs of matching, step-shoulder, brick chimneys that once framed the slate gable roof.

In 1787, the front steps, the wide gallery porches at the front and back entrances, and the piers the house rested on were custom fitted from locally quarried stone. Each rock positioned by hand and locked in place with strong mortar made with slaked lime and sand dug from the marl pits and sand barrens located near Nahunta Swamp, which formed the northern property line.

"This foundation will stand forever," Hub would say, "but it's what happens in the rooms above that tests our fate."

Lottie didn't want to be sorry he was dead. She didn't want to wish she had spoken to him one more time.

"What good would it have done," Lottie whispered and clucked to the mare to move on.

When it was built, the two-story rectangular shaped manor, modeled on Federal-style architecture with balconies and pillared porches, looked out on nearly two thousand acres of Edwards's land. Back when money flowed freely into the family coffers, the plantation was a showcase of antebellum excess. Today, most of the land had been sold off. All of what lay at the top of the hand-laid steps had been reduced to a pile of smoldering rubble. A portion of the grand staircase stood in the middle of the debris, appearing as a scorched appendage reaching out of the charred remains.

Out of habit, Lottie rode the mare down the decline of the carriage drive to the back of the main house. She was never allowed to use the front door. Patrick and Patrice followed. No one spoke. Lottie dismounted and tied the mare to the hitching post. She pulled the knife from her saddlebag and sliced the rope that attached the pole-sled to the saddle. Lottie dropped Calvin's body on the ground at his burned-out backdoor.

Then she started for the house.

"Where are you going?" Patrice asked.

"I need to see if it's here," Lottie explained.

Patrice dismounted. "If what is here?"

Patrick remained in the saddle, warily looking at the empty barns and stables.

He asked, "Don't you think it is too quiet, eerily so?"

Lottie climbed the back steps and saw that the main floor remained intact in most places, though the walls were burned down to the baseboards. She answered Patrick, as she carefully placed her boot on the hardwood floor.

"I imagine everyone left when Hub sold all the horses. Maybe he turned out the slaves too. This is, or was, a horse farm. Without horses, there isn't a lot to do."

Patrick stayed in the saddle and searched the horizon.

"They haven't been gone long," he commented. "If the house had not burned, no one would know the place was abandoned."

Patrice followed Lottie up the back steps. "As I recall, Delphia said Hub would rather sell his stock to a breeder in South America than see the bloodlines tarnished by Wade Hampton's studs. She said Harriet thought Hub was going to go with them."

Patrick remained vigilant, as he commented, "Hub had his breeding standards, and South America might not be a bad place to be if this war keeps going."

"It's over," Patrice said. "The Confederacy States of America are finished, even if Jeff Davis won't admit it." She stopped behind Lottie and asked, "What are you looking for?"

Lottie had taken only a few steps into what was the main hallway before she stopped. At her feet lay a pair of boots and what appeared to be charred legs sticking out from under a smoldering pile of debris.

Patrice peeked around Lottie at the floor. "Oh, my. Is that—"

"I don't know. It could be. He was the only person in the house, from what Patrick said."

Patrice stepped in front of Lottie for a closer look, appalled but curious it seemed. But then Lottie learned inquisitiveness wasn't what had propelled Patrice forward at all.

Patrice called to her brother, "Patrick, you should come here."

"What is it? What do you see?" Lottie asked, staring at the boots for a clue.

Patrick bounded up the stairs, still wary. "Ladies, this isn't exactly safe, wandering around in a still burning structure, with— Oh, I see."

Patrick froze at the sight of the boots.

"What? What is it?" Lottie demanded.

"That isn't your father, Lottie," Patrice said. "That's Gabriel. I recognize his spurs."

"Jack will be on the warpath over this," Patrick added.

"If that's Gabriel, where is Hub?" Lottie asked, peering around the piles of smoking wreckage. She turned to Patrice. "Stay here. You're not really dressed for walking around in a fire."

Patrice reached for Lottie's hand and gave it a squeeze. "Be careful."

Lottie smiled. In the middle of looking for her father's remains, she smiled at Patrice. The highs and lows of living in a war zone had to be taken as they came. Lottie shook her head at the absurdity of her situation and moved further into the house. The library had burned, every book a charred pile of dust. The mantel and hearth, built out of the same stone as the steps, were all that remained standing in Lottie's favorite room of her father's home. She approached the fireplace and held her hand out over the rock.

"The fire was yesterday before twilight, and the hearth is still too warm to touch. This was a big fire. A lot of people would have seen the flames."

"Most people have their own problems or are too scared to venture far from home," Patrice said. "Do you see any sign of your father?"

Lottie used the knife to pry up a flat stone on the corner of the hearth, exposing a tin box. She knew about the box because of her time hiding in the library as a child. James was right about her. She could keep a secret. The box was warm, but not too hot to lift out of its hiding place. The disappointment must have shown when Lottie lifted the lid to find the box empty.

Patrice asked, "What was there but isn't now?"

Lottie threw the box down. "He kept important papers, deeds and such, in there. I used to sneak in and look at them. He either gave the papers to Harriet or he died with them in his pocket somewhere under one of these piles of smoldering ash."

"I'm not so sure about that," Patrick said.

He had moved some of the fallen plaster off Gabriel's body. He looked over at Patrice.

"Sister, in your duties at the hospital, I suppose you've learned quite a bit. Would you say that is a bullet hole between our half-brother's eyes?"

Patrice leaned around one brother to take a gander at the other. Her hand flew to cover her nose and mouth. She nodded her agreement with Patrick's assessment.

He handed Patrice a handkerchief, with which she quickly covered her nose.

Lottie walked back to the twins with careful steps and then onto the stone back porch.

"What happened here?" Lottie asked the question aloud, but to no one in particular. "Where is my father?"

Patrick again surveyed the surroundings. "I don't know where your father is, but I see two fresh holes dug in the family plot, which I believe means we are not alone."

A bright blue spring sky filled with the black silhouettes of turkey buzzards waiting their turn at the carnage. The air over Wayne County teemed with them.

"Well, we got two bodies and two holes, so I guess we should use them and keep the buzzards from a meal." Lottie started down the steps toward Calvin. "Might as well start with this one. Then we can use the blanket to gather Gabriel."

"Lottie, did you hear Patrick? He doesn't think we're alone."

"Who would dig a hole for Gabriel?" Lottie asked. "I don't know who the second hole is for, but I imagine it's for Hub Edwards. Whoever dug those holes, isn't going to kill me, at least not until I finish the job for him."

"Lottie," Patrick called after her, "if it's a friend, why are they still hiding?"

"Because that is Jack Cole's son in there with a bullet hole in his forehead, and you are Cole's children."

Patrice waved the handkerchief her brother had given her in the air and shouted, "If you are out there, none of us care that either of these men is dead. We'll bury them, which is only Christian, and be on our way."

Lottie chuckled. "Despite your sophistication, your naiveté is amusing."

"Why do you say that?" Patrice implored.

Lottie continued her task, untying Calvin's shrouded body from the sled, while she answered, "You assume a person who might kill two women and a man to remain anonymous, would heed your white flag declaration."

"Go down there and help her, Patrick," Patrice ordered, and then returned to Lottie's argument. "I contend telling whoever is out there that we mean no harm is better than letting them wonder why we're here."

"Then you stay up there and keep a lookout for signs of a misunderstanding," Lottie stated, not offering Patrice much choice.

Patrick removed his frock coat and placed it over his horse's saddle. "Are you sure you want to have her around to boss you about, Lottie?"

"I don't intend to be led around by the nose," Lottie answered, confidently.

Patrick huffed at Lottie's bravado. "You told me when you left a thing it stayed left, but alas, there she stands. Patrice set the ring in your nose fast and deep."

Lottie glared at Patrick. "Take hold of his feet and pull him out of this blanket."

"How do you even know this is him? He has a bag over his head."

"Did you hear of any other white men strung up last night? Besides, he has that brandy-wine stain on the top of his foot. I remember it from when we were kids. It's Calvin. Quit stalling and help me."

Patrick grumbled, "I did not plan on touching dead men today. I am hopeful of warmer exchanges, but dead cold was not in my plan."

As Patrick bent to grab Calvin's feet, Lottie asked, "So, did you really get caught with the sharecropper's son? Did Jack beat you until Patrice stopped him?"

"They don't teach discretion in Bratcher Patch, do they?"

"I think we're beyond having questions of one another, Mr. Cole. We'll be bearing each other's secrets from here out, I suspect."

Patrick stopped helping slide the blanket out from under the body of Calvin Edwards and stared at Lottie.

Lottie answered his questioning expression with, "I only ask because there is so much lore surrounding the two of you. Who knows what the truth is?"

Patrick bent again to help Lottie drag Calvin to the open holes near an old family graveyard dotted with a century's worth of rotting wooden markers.

"I was nearly killed by Jack upon being discovered embracing someone for whom I care deeply. His displeasure at my behavior obliged him to force himself on me. The sharecropper's son was a dear boy, but not my lover. My sister did save my life. Dr. Davis sewed me back together, and when I was healed, Patrice and I went away at the behest of our Grandmother Cane. We came back only because our inheritance is not ours to have, as of yet, and the only home we have is where we are currently living. Now, you know the truth of it."

"I would have killed him, Patrick," Lottie said, as she noticed Calvin's hands looked much like their father's.

"When the time comes," Patrick said, with a casualness Lottie recognized as resolute decisiveness.

"It is a curse to know we can never have what we love," Lottie said, surprised by her candor.

"The creator placed in each of us a unique passion for the soul that makes us whole. The choice is made for us. My grandmother told me so, and I choose to believe her explanation of things."

"I don't figure I've spent much time thinking about it," Lottie commented. "I reckon Patrice was put here to torment me, to be sure."

Patrick laughed. "You may as well give in to her, Lottie. She can be relentless."

They reached the graveyard with Calvin's body. One grave was dug deep enough. The other appeared as though the digging had been interrupted. Lottie and Patrick both surveyed their surroundings again.

"Are you going to leave that noose around his neck?" Patrick asked.

Lottie looked down at her half-brother's body and smirked. "Leave it. The devil will know what he's dealing with when he gets there."

"I told Patrice you had a cold heart."

Lottie leaned down and rolled Calvin Edwards into the open grave. "He chose to torment the rest of his family, to flaunt his heir-apparent status, to chastise us as unworthy of his father's name—may he rot."

"Why didn't you just leave him to swing?"

"I can tell his mother where to find him. She'll have the deed to half of Bratcher Patch now. A kindness might have some sway."

Lottie stepped over to the other hole. A spade lay beside the pile of dirt removed from the grave.

"I'll make this deeper. See if you and Patrice can get Gabriel in that gum blanket."

Lottie jumped down in the hole and immediately knew something was wrong. "What in the hell?"

Patrick peered down at her. "What is it?"

Lottie poked the loose dirt at her feet with the spade. "There is something under here." She knelt down and moved dirt away with her hand. "Sweet Jesus!"

Lottie jumped out of the grave like a frog off a hot pan.

Patrick took a reflexive step back. "What's down there?"

Lottie pointed down in the hole. Patrick leaned over to see for himself. She patted him on the shoulder.

"You don't have to worry about taking another beating from Jack."

At the bottom of the hole where Lottie swept away the soil, Jack Cole's dead eyeball stared up at them.

"We need to go."

Patrice's voice reached them almost simultaneously with the sound of hoof beats.

She was clamoring down the back stairs as she said again, "We need to go, now."

Lottie and Patrick made a run for the horses.

"Don't mount," Lottie said quietly. "Follow me."

Lottie led the mare down the incline behind the main house. The approaching riders would not see them as they descended the hill and slipped behind the large barn. When she and the twins were safely out of sight, Lottie pointed to a path leading into densely wooded lowland.

"There is a ford back there. Hub laid limestone slabs across a shallow section of Nahunta Swamp. You can cross there. Follow this leg of the swamp northwest, and you'll run into Faro in about three miles. "

A muzzle blast close by startled the people and the horses huddled behind the barn. Answering shots came from up by the house.

Patrice instinctively dropped to her knees. Lottie reached under her elbow and pulled Patrice back into standing position.

"You'll get stomped down there. Stay up close to the horse. Be ready to mount."

Patrick stared into the swamp. Lottie could hear men and horses all around them. No one, at the moment, was actually shooting at them. She drew the pistol from her waist and waited for a chance to leave the battlefield they found themselves in. The opposing forces did not appear to care that she and the Cole twins were there.

Patrice locked her eyes on Lottie's, watching her for cues. Lottie knew she had to get them out of there. Since the people in the swamp could see them and were not shooting at them, Lottie thought that was probably their best option. Patrick apparently made the same decision.

"Let's go!" he shouted.

Lottie saw that he too had produced a pistol. She glanced at Patrice.

"Are you ready?"

Patrice nodded that she was.

"See that break in the trees. You go through there and do not look back. Mount up."

Lottie made sure Patrice was seated before she tended to her own mount. Patrick was already in his saddle.

"Don't let her follow me," Lottie said, just before she slapped Patrice's horse on the rump. "Ha!"

The bay needed no further prodding. She and Patrick's mount took off for the woods. Lottie hopped into the mare's saddle and bolted in the other direction, paralleling the swamp, drawing fire. Lottie stood in the stirrups, bent her knees, leaned over the mare's neck, and asked her for all she had. The filly was tired, but also petrified. With the heart of a prey animal in flight, she answered Lottie's call with the speed Hub Edwards bred into her.

Lottie glanced back to see that the Cole twins had disappeared into the cloaking thick forest. She was shocked, however, to see a horse gaining on her until she realized who it was. Big John was coming for his girl, with Jefferson holding on for his life.

She whistled to him and kicked the mare for more. They tore away from the fighting, leaving nothing but puffs of dust as hooves tore across a hard packed pasture. Lottie could hear Jefferson laughing when he finally pulled up in the shadows of the forest five hundred yards from the main house, with Lottie right behind him.

"Damn fine horse," he said.

Big John pawed the ground and snorted at Lottie. He pranced and tossed his head in disproval of her absence.

"Hello, my boy. That was a good run, right? Good boy!" Lottie rubbed the big horse's neck. "Jefferson, how the hell did you end up at Pa's in the middle of a shootout?"

"I could ask you the same thing," Jefferson said, looking in the direction from whence they came.

"I brought Calvin's body home. The Yankees strung him up. They left a sign on him warning Jack and the rest of the home patrols to give the Yankees a wide berth. I suppose you should have heeded that advice."

"The men we were following are not Yankees. It's that Tiller fella."

Lottie dismounted and peered across the open pasture to the Edwards's place. The rifle and pistol fire was sporadic now. The battle had quieted.

Lottie turned to Jefferson. "Who is 'we'? Who fired that rifle? I don't think Tiller knew we were there."

"He knew. One of his men was sneaking down to the barn. I don't know who shot him, but his sneaking days are over." Jefferson stepped up beside her. "Eli, Deland, and Joshua are out there. James's boys are out there too."

"You brought Ethan and Nathan with you?"

"Hold on, now. Brought would mean I knew those boys were following us. You see all hell broke loose around here after you left with Harper. We didn't know what happened to you and—"

Lottie put her hand up asking for silence. They listened, before Lottie said, "Sounds like the fight is over or the powder ran out." She then turned to Jefferson. "Jack Cole is in a grave up there by the house. Gabriel is in the house with a bullet hole between his eyes. Do you know anything about that?"

"No, Charlie went back to Bratcher Patch. Tiller was there again. James and the womenfolk sent him packing, but he promised to burn the place down if you didn't show up soon with 'his horse.' Charlie came back, told us what happened, and then went back to help James protect the Patch. We decided instead of sittin' and waitin' on Tiller to do his worst, we'd run him to ground. James's boys came on their own accord before we knew they were there."

"The Yankees bumped into Jack out here last night. This is where they got Calvin. I was told Hub died in that fire, but Jack survived. His body is still warm, so I think he was shot not long ago."

"We saw the blaze last night, heard the shooting, but we stuck right to Tiller. It wasn't him that killed Jack. I know that for sure. Tiller has four, maybe five men left, but he won't leave the field. He's run in circles up here, looking for something."

"I think he just found it," Lottie said, pointing out at the pasture, "and he always has more men. As long as he has silver, he'll have men."

Tiller galloped to within a hundred yards and brought his horse to a rearing stop at a spot in the pasture where the land fell away sharply. The geographical feature created a trough for a natural spring. This fall line demarked an ancient sea floor, which gradually descended to the marl beds beyond the trees. It was also dangerous for anyone who didn't know it was there, which was the reason Lottie and Jefferson rode around it in hopes pursuers would not.

Tiller grinned, "Giiirrrrllll," he yelled. "I almost fell in your trap." He laughed and coaxed his horse down the embankment to flat land again. "I know you're in them trees. Come out. The hounds have run the fox to ground. Give up, girly. You got no way out."

Jefferson whispered, "That pistol, is it loaded?"

"Where's yours?" Lottie asked.

Jefferson held open his pistol. "I shot my wads worth. I don't have anything to reload with."

Tiller kept yelling. "I'm talking to ya', giiirrrlll. They shot four of my men in Goldsborough today on your word. I can't let that stand. I'll take that horse in a fair trade."

Tiller's statement puzzled Lottie. "How does he know that? Did you see any other riders come from town?"

Jefferson shook his head. "Only you and the twins."

Lottie handed over the Colt to Jefferson. "I got four cylinders ready, but I loaded them in a while back. You might want to tamp it down again. I can't swear to dry powder, nor that the caps are seated. I used lard for ball grease. Keep shooting 'til she fires, would be my policy."

Jefferson looked the pistol over. "How much powder? Paper wad or poured yourself?"

"James loaded it, twenty grain, I believe. He made the wads too. Said I could hit a deer at fifty yards easy, seventy-five if I shot steady."

"How does she shoot? Does it carry high?"

"I shot it once. We had no powder to practice. The Confederate government took everything from us while you were gone, Jeff."

Tiller continued his taunts. "I know your back is to the swamp and it's too deep and muddy to cross there. You'll lose that horse to the marl clay if you try to swim it. If you come out on that road there, you'll lose your life to me."

Jefferson didn't seem concerned with the hardships of home life during the war. He focused solely on surviving, which is why he was still alive, Lottie surmised.

Exasperated, he challenged his sister, "Did you hit what you aimed for?"

"Yes, it shoots true, as I recall. What are you going to do, Jeff?"

Tiller's tone changed, and he tried a new threat. "We can wait here for the Yankees if you like. I'm sure they'll want to know who put Jack Cole in that grave and the bullet in his son's head."

Lottie answered back. "Jack Cole left here alive last night. Now, he's dead, and you're here. The Yankees might want to talk to you, Mr. Tiller."

"The Yankees might want to hang some of those deserters chasing me all night. What do you know about those fellas, Miss Lottie Bratcher?"

"I'm going to shoot that man right between the eyes," Jefferson said.

Lottie followed Jefferson's gaze to Tiller. In the manner that evil men seem to have, the grizzled, outlaw nodded toward the thicket on his right and played his trump card at the appropriate last moment.

"The thing about running from vigilantes and deserters is you folks got nothing left. Eventually, you run out of powder and volunteers. Whereas, I have plenty cap and ball to spare."

From the thicket, a man drove Ethan and Nathan out in front of his horse. Their hands were tied behind their backs with a rope drawing them together, the other end of which wrapped around the saddle horn of Tiller's man's horse.

Lottie called out to Tiller. "I see you and one other. You're gambling I have no ball left. Come closer and play your cards."

"I can offer a piece of silver and have four more just like the ones what faced the firing squad in town today. I'm not a man to trifle with."

"I'd pocket my coin and drink my share before I rode a step for you, Tiller," Jefferson said. "You are like the armies driving good men to sure death."

Tiller sneered. "Ah, now there's the voice of a deserter. War is 'sure death.' You don't get to go home because you don't like your odds."

Lottie shouted, "I don't see the color of your uniform. You serve no flag. You're a thief and so are your men."

Ethan chimed in, "I helped burn two of them myself."

Tiller's man kicked Ethan in the back, sending him sprawling face first in the dirt.

Nathan fell down next to his brother and screamed, "Leave him alone."

"Two boys and a deserter. That's what came to your rescue. That deserter in there with you must be kin. You can forget those others. They high-tailed it after that pretty girl and her brother. That rebel whore will get her comeuppance. I'll get to her when I'm done with you."

Lottie faced Jefferson. "Give me your pistol."

"But it's empty."

"Tiller doesn't know that."

Jefferson handed Lottie his weapon.

"Hit what you aim at, Jeff. We can't let that man leave here alive. He'll be too focused on me to notice you."

Lottie sprang to her feet. She hooked a toe in a stirrup and hopped into Big John's saddle. She looked down at Jefferson.

"I'm going to come up on the other side of the one with the boys tied on his horse. Send the mare out in front of you. When Tiller turns to shoot at me, kill him."

"But, Lottie, we don't know for sure how many men he has lef—"

"I suppose we are about to find out. Ha!" Lottie yelled and tightened her knees around Big John. As she cleared the trees, she shouted at her nephews, "Run, boys! Run!"

167

Ethan and Nathan scrambled to their feet and started running. Naturally, the horse and Tiller's man on the other end of the rope pulled back, but the distraction served its purpose. The rider did not get off a shot at Lottie.

Pow! Zzzipft!

The man holding her nephews didn't fire, but somebody did. The rider slumped over, as Lottie galloped past him.

Lottie lowered her head and kept riding as fast as Big John could go. He had an explosive start, but his speed came in long distance.

Bang! Pftzzzzz!

A bullet whizzed by Lottie's head. She looked up to see a third man directly ahead, exploding out of the forest on her left. Lottie and Big John became as one, every muscle of their bodies in concert. Thundering through the pasture, they charged straight at the approaching man.

The rider raised his pistol to fire again as Lottie grew nearer, but nothing happened. He seemed to freeze there for a moment. His arm dropped first, and then his body fell from his horse.

Lottie turned Big John in a wide circle, intent on returning to rescue her nephews and help Jefferson if necessary. Two more men, unseen until now, charged from the road.

Pow! Psssfttt! Bang! Zzzzzftt!

Projectiles whizzed through the air. Lottie found herself in the crossfire.

"Wooo-whoooo-eey!"

"Yeeee-haaaaa!"

"Yayayayayaya-eeeee!"

From the swamp, where Lottie had sent the twins, came a commotion fit for a force twice its size, with Patrice right in the thick of the rest of the Appletree Swamp gang. Powder and ball shortage aside, Deland and Joshua blazed away with pistols, while Eli leveled a rifle at Tiller's men.

Patrick had apparently surrendered his weapon to one of the soldiers. He brandished a large knife and looked quite dashing, if not terribly menacing. His sister courageously held a two-shot derringer out in front of her while in full gallop. That pistol wasn't likely to do any damage from a distance, but the jaw set of Miss Cole threatened a killing if the opportunity arose.

Lottie found herself in the lead of the charging swamp cavalry, headed right at Tiller's men. The only weapons Lottie had were an unloaded pistol and Big John. Tiller was somewhere on her right now, hopefully dead. She glanced that way for an answer to her question. It was not the outcome for which Lottie had hoped.

Tiller sat on his horse on the other side of the fall off. From her position nearer the road, Lottie could not see who was on the ground in front of him, but she could definitely make out the pistol in Tiller's hand aimed in that direction.

"Oh, sweet Jesus," Lottie said and turned Big John hard to the right.

Both the swamp cavalry and Tiller's men turned with her. Now, Lottie led both her allies and enemies back across the pasture, hooves thundering, shots ringing out. Lottie threw the empty pistol at one of Tiller's men. She missed, but now her hands were free.

She focused ahead, leaned into Big John, and yelled to him, "Go, boy! Go!"

They made this jump many times in his younger years when Lottie and Big John were frequent visitors to this pasture. The horse under her readied for his part, she felt his gate change, and then they were flying, stretched out over the man on the horse below. Big John's hind legs raked Tiller from his saddle.

Horse and rider landed soundly. Lottie turned in time to see the next horse over the ledge held Patrick Cole in the saddle. He and the bay made a beautiful picture of equestrian majesty. Tiller recovered from landing on the ground and scrambled to his feet. He should have stayed down.

Patrick came over the jump with his hand high above his head, the knife he held glinting in the sun. With the grace of a practiced knife thrower, on his way by the startled man, Patrick let loose the knife and sent it into Tiller's chest. Seeing this, his remaining two men broke off their engagement and retreated towards Goldsborough. Eli pulled his horse up, jumped off, and dropped to one knee. He sighted the escaping men and pulled the trigger on the rifle. One rider tumbled from his horse. A second shot came from somewhere. The last of Tiller's men fell.

Tiller looked down and clutched at the knife as a red stain formed across his chest. He looked up at Lottie and Patrick. "Done in by a fancy-man and a woman in trousers."

Tiller dropped to his knees and then keeled over on his face, just as the rest of the swamp gang stopped their mounts.

Jefferson, who had been huddled with his nephews under Tiller's gun, spoke first. "Patrick, as usual, your timing is impeccable."

Patrick tipped the brim of his hat, "Thank you."

Jefferson spoke next to Lottie, "Your pistol pulls high and to the right."

Lottie smiled with relief. "I suppose that's your way of explaining why Tiller was still alive."

Jefferson pointed at the man who had been holding the rope tied to the boys. "I hit the first one."

Patrice rode up beside Lottie, but she spoke to Patrick. She looked shaken and was stern in tone. "There could be more. We need to dispense with any clue of what just happened here."

Jefferson gave an order to Deland and Joshua, "Ride out a way. See what you can see."

The two nodded and rode away. Ethan and Nathan had escaped their bonds and stood clinging to one another, trembling and crying, their faces showing enlightenment toward the bloodiness of war fairly earned.

Jefferson spoke to them, "Boys, I know you're scared. We all are, but we have work to do. Go with Eli and gather those dead riders' horses. Take them back into the swamp where we came out. Stay back up in there until we come to get you. Make sure you find all their weapons and cartridges."

"We will, Uncle Jeff," Ethan said.

"We'll mind from now on," Nathan said, between sniffles.

All the adults let out a chuckle, a much-needed release of tensions.

"I expect you will," Jefferson said, as he adjusted Nathan's hat.

Eli started off with the boys but turned after a few steps. "Jeff, who shot that second fella?"

"I don't know, but seeing as how he hasn't shot one of us, I think he must be on our side."

"Good thing the twins had a stash of powder and shot in their saddle bags. Well, if you find the man that took that second rider down, tell him that was a hell of a shot," Eli said with a smile and then took off after the boys.

Lottie looked back toward the big barn. Patrick followed her gaze.

"I told you someone was watching us," he said.

"Well, I hope they don't mind watching this next part and being quiet about it," Lottie answered. "I'll get this one."

Patrick balked. "This day does drag on—more dead men. I look forward to delving into Grandmother's hidden brandy reserves this evening."

Jefferson walked over to Uncle William's mare and mounted up. He came close to his sister. Lottie opened the mare's saddlebag and took out her knife. She set about cutting the rope that once held her nephews, while Jefferson talked with the Coles.

"You're rid of Jack. That brandy will taste sweeter knowing that."

Patrick grinned at Jefferson. "I should like to buy the fellow who pulled that trigger a well-deserved drink. If you see him, tell him he is welcome in my parlor anytime."

Lottie took a piece of the rope and gave the rest to Jefferson. She tied one end around Tiller's ankles.

"What goes in the marl pit doesn't come out, and that's just the grave I think Mr. Tiller and his henchmen deserve."

"We'll get the other four," Jefferson said.

He and Patrick moved off together. Patrice and Lottie were finally alone.

Lottie yelled after them, "Don't forget that fifth one up by the barn."

"Lottie?" Patrice said, still seated on her horse.

Lottie answered as she tied Tiller's body off to Big John's saddle horn. "I know I upset you this morning. We can talk about—"

Patrice interrupted her. "Is that your father talking to your nephews?"

Lottie turned to look where Patrice pointed. A tall man carrying a long rifle stood by the barn a short distance from Eli and the boys. The man took one more step and collapsed.

Chapter Twenty-Two

Let Him Rot

"…earth to earth, ashes to ashes, dust to dust; looking for the general Resurrection in the last day, and the life of the world to come, through our Lord Jesus Christ, Amen."

"Amen," came from those gathered at the now covered gravesites.

"Amen," repeated the Yankee captain standing behind them.

Everyone showed the appropriate solemnity for the circumstance, although the captain appeared suspicious. Lottie continued to be impressed with how Patrice had orchestrated the charade. There was much more to Patrice Cole than beauty, as Lottie was learning.

A few seconds after Hub Edwards had hit the ground in front of his grandsons, Deland and Joshua had returned from reconnaissance, blazing a path down the road. They stuck to the grass on the edge of the path so as not to leave a cloud of dust behind.

"The Yankees are coming," Joshua yelled as he reined his horse to a stop near Patrice and Lottie. "You have about ten minutes."

Patrice immediately said, "Go! Help get the others. I'll drag this one." She took the rope Lottie held, the one tied around Tiller's ankles, and shouted, "Hurry!"

Lottie thought Patrice was more afraid of the Yankees than she had been of Tiller's men. She didn't have time to ask why. Deland had ridden on to where Jeff and Patrick were. Everyone was soon involved in moving bodies into the marl pit.

The nephews were still with Eli and the fallen Hub, when Lottie and the rest of the gang finished erasing the signs of the recent battle. The whole process took about five minutes.

"Here, take all the weapons and get those horses out of here," Jefferson shouted at Eli. "Deland and Joshua, you go with Eli and the boys. Get back to the camp. Charlie will be coming for news. Let him know I'm with Lottie. No matter what happens next, do not come back here. Go, and quickly. Hide your trail as best you can."

The nephews did not need to be told twice. Wide-eyed and terrified, they had enough of war to last them their lifetimes, if facial expressions meant anything. They mounted two horses and rode off into the swamp. The others followed.

While the gang moved off, Patrice went to kneel beside Hub Edwards. "He needs water. I think he's been shot." She pulled back his outer coat and looked under it. "He has a wound in the shoulder."

"If the Yankees see him like that, they might put it together that he was here last night," Lottie said. "Can you help him, Patrice?"

"No, the bullet has to come out. He already has a fever." Patrice shook Hub's unwounded shoulder. "Mr. Edwards, can you hear me?"

She received no response.

Patrick asked Patrice, "What should we do with Gabriel's body?"

Patrice stood and began giving orders. "You and Jefferson get Gabriel's body and put it in the hole with Jack. They were meant to be together for eternity. Cover the graves. Hurry!" She turned to Lottie. "Get the gum blanket."

Lottie did as the other two and followed Patrice's instructions without question. She came back with the blanket. Patrice had stripped the frock coat off Hub by the time she returned.

"Now what?"

"Help me put him on the blanket. We're going to use it to slide him over by the graves."

Lottie hesitated. "He's a bastard, Patrice, but we're not going to bury him alive."

"Lottie, I'm trying to save his life. Please just help me. I don't have time to explain."

Lottie's options were limited, so she followed instructions.

Patrice called to her brother. "Bring the prayer book and the pencil stub from my saddlebag."

Lottie helped move her father onto the blanket. She commented to Patrice, "A lot has changed about him since I last saw his face."

"I'm sure if he was able, he would say the same," Patrice said, as she threw Hub's coat on the blanket with him.

"Seven years, four of those at war, a lot has changed about all of us. I find it hard to remember when we were carefree children."

Once Hub was situated on the blanket, Lottie and Patrice pulled him over to the gravesites. Lottie joined Jefferson in pushing dirt into the graves. Patrick brought the bible and pencil to Patrice. He also brought a plank of charred wood to help move the dirt. Patrice sat down on the blanket beside Hub.

Lottie commented, "I don't think now is the time to start praying for a dying man. We're all going to die if the Yankees find him here."

"Move dirt, Lottie. Let Patrice be," Jefferson said.

Her brother's response caught Lottie off guard.

"One of you tell me what I'm to do, because the Yankees are breaking out the woods and headed our way," Lottie said, as she spotted the blue coats just five hundred yards away.

Patrice stood up from the blanket and walked over to the burial crew. "Play the part of the concerned daughter. You can do that can't you?"

"Yes, but—"

Patrice cut Lottie off, "Jefferson, this is your paroled prisoner pass. You were exchanged after Gettysburg. Rub it in your hands, crumple it, get it dirty, and then fold it and put it in your pocket." She gave Jefferson his father's coat. "Put this on. Wearing it you should not look so much like you have been living in the swamp for months."

Jefferson kissed Patrice on the cheek, a familiarity that also shocked Lottie.

Patrice handed the Book of Common Prayer to her brother. "You'll do the reading, page two-seventy, at the bottom."

Patrick laughed. "I would rather dance a jig at Jack's demise than pray over his corpse. I often wished for him to burn in hell. It seems rather hypocritical of me to pray for his soul."

Lottie nodded. "I feel the same way about Calvin. Good riddance."

"Shhh!" Patrice hissed. When she had their attention, she said, "If you must lie, stay close to the truth. If all goes well, we'll be in Goldsborough for brandy at sundown."

"And if it doesn't go well?" Lottie asked under her breath.

The hoof beats closed in.

Patrick bowed his head and said, "Let us pray."

Patrice bowed her head and reached for Lottie's hand. She whispered, "Then I should tell you that I love you, before I'm robbed of the chance."

"For as much as it hath pleased the Almighty God, in his wise providence, to take out of this world the soul of our deceased brethren, we therefore commit his body to the ground..."

Patrick bent to pick up a handful of loose soil and tossed it onto the graves. The rest of the party did the same in full view of the Yankee patrol, whose horses snorted and pranced behind them.

Patrick continued as if they were not there, "...earth to earth, ashes to ashes, dust to dust; looking for the general Resurrection in the last day, and the life of the world to come, through our Lord Jesus Christ, Amen."

"Amen," came from those gathered at the now covered gravesites.

"Amen," repeated Captain Fleischer.

Patrick closed the prayer book and turned to the captain. "Captain Fleischer, how Christian of you to stop for the internment."

Captain Fleischer was focused on Lottie, "Who's in those holes?"

Lottie answered. "This one is the man you strung up, Calvin Edwards. The other grave, we put in the two we found in the rubble, already dead."

Lottie left Jack and Gabriel's names out of her description. She thought Patrice probably had a story to cover them.

"I thought you said you didn't know that fella last night."

"I don't know him. He is my father's son, but my mother lived in the servants quarters, while his lived in the big house," Lottie said, and then smiled wickedly. "Me and the quarters are still standing."

"Who is this?" The captain pointed at Hub.

"That's my father," Lottie said.

"How did he come to be shot? Is he patrol like his son?"

Jefferson answered, "No, sir. He is a pacifist. His sons had other ideas."

The captain became interested in Jefferson, "And why are you not in uniform."

"I was paroled after Gettysburg. I was wounded and then sent home. There will be no more war for me. I've seen enough."

The captain pointed at Patrick, who had obviously undergone his questioning before. "He has a medical parole from the war. The Rebs have boys fighting. Why would they leave you home? You look well enough."

"You should have seen him when he came home. He was a bag of bones with the bloody flux and a weeping wound," Lottie said. "I can pull more weight on the farm than he can, now."

She had read the diaries. Lottie knew what Jefferson went through to get well. The captain needed further documentation of Jefferson's story.

"Let me see your parole papers, or are you going to say they are at home in a lock box, like every other deserter we've come upon."

"A man would be foolish in these times not to carry parole papers," Jefferson said, as he fished the document from the inside pocket of the frock coat.

Captain Fleischer examined the paper carefully. "Paroled out of Satterlee General Hospital in Philadelphia. Sent home on the train straight to Goldsboro, I suppose?"

Patrice still held Lottie's hand. Lottie felt her grip tighten when the captain asked Jefferson the question.

"Had to go through Norfolk for the exchange," Jefferson answered.

Patrice loosed her grasp on Lottie with Jefferson's answer. Lottie supposed the question was meant to trip him on a lie, but he evidently knew the right answer. The captain handed him the parole paper and returned his attention to Hub.

"This man, none of you know how he was shot?"

It was time for Patrice to weave her tale. She let go of Lottie's hand and moved closer to the Captain. It was then that Lottie saw the single tear on Patrice's cheek.

"Captain Fleischer, the two men in the grave are my father, Jack Cole, and my half-brother, Gabriel. As you are well aware, Jack ran the patrols in Wayne County. You are also aware that my brother and I did not live with Jack nor share his views. I suspect Jack used his activities in the patrol to disguise a personal motive. This smells of a land deal gone wrong and nothing to do with war."

"Jack Cole came here to kill me."

Everyone in attendance shifted attention to the man on the blanket. Lottie had not heard him speak in seven years. She could hear the age in his voice but he sounded the same. Jefferson moved to his father's side. Lottie remained frozen in place.

The captain asked, "Did you kill him?"

"Yes, he came while I was digging graves for his son and mine. I knew Calvin was hung. I meant to go get him and bury him here for his mother before I left."

"Where were you going Pa?"

Hub coughed a bit before he smiled weakly and said, "I'm going home, son."

The captain asked, "Where's home?"

"Bratcher Patch," Hub answered.

Lottie was finally stirred to move. "I'll be damned if that's so."

Hub tried to sit up but couldn't. "Charlotte, you don't understand," he managed to say before he began to cough again.

"Yes, I do. You paid the taxes on the Patch and now you're going to take the only thing my mother has left. I wish Jack had killed you."

"Lottie!" Jefferson objected to Lottie's bluntness.

"Enough!" Captain Fleischer shook his head. "Ladies and gentlemen, I much prefer this family disagreement take place elsewhere. There are rebels in this area and a fight is sure to come. This man needs a doctor. Take him to Goldsborough and get out of the fray."

Lottie stomped off toward Big John. Once in the saddle, she looked back at everyone on the ground. "He can rot there."

Patrice called to her, "Lottie wait."

"Ha!" Lottie barked and Big John responded.

Lottie couldn't wait. She wouldn't give Hub Edwards the satisfaction of watching her cry.

Chapter Twenty-Three

Miracles Happen

Lottie had traveled about two and a half miles when she finally let Big John out of the trot. She was halfway home and could see the steeple on the Faro church above the trees. When she rounded the last turn before the crossroads, she made an unexpected discovery.

"Now, what?"

Coming down the road toward her, it appeared a large faction of her family had loaded up in the old two-box wagon, attached a horse she did not recognize to an old set of traces, and were on their way to Bullhead. James was holding the reins and standing in the box wagon, with John Simpson next to him with a rifle in hand.

Lottie stopped Big John and waited for the wagon to approach. When it was closer, she could see Martha Ann and Avery May standing behind the other two.

"Lottie, where's Pa?" James asked, as soon as he was in range.

"Dead, I hope," Lottie answered.

James kept the wagon moving, and Lottie fell in beside them.

Avery May shouted, "Don't say that."

"It's good to see you too, Avery, but why would my father's condition concern you?"

"He kept me safe all these months, fed me, hid me in his barn."

Martha Ann beamed with joy. "Pa saved my Avery, Lottie. I told you he was coming home. Now, we have to help Pa."

Avery explained further, "Lottie, your father saved me, but he saved a lot more when he put that bullet in Jack Cole this morning. He was going to string me up for a deserter. He said so. I was digging Cole's grave when Tiller's men came through. We hid Jack's horse and us in the swamp, back of the barn. By then your Pa was beginning to fail on account of where Gabriel shot him in the shoulder. I thought I better get some help, so I put your Pa in the hayloft with his Whitworth rifle and took Jack's horse to Bratcher Patch."

James spoke next, "Lottie, it's time you put away your childish anger."

Lottie felt the flush of her ire. "Why didn't anyone tell me he paid the taxes on the land? Now, he's taking Bratcher Patch, James. He is taking everything."

John Simpson said, to Lottie's amazement, "He didn't take it. He gave Jane her part and put the rest in your name, Charlotte. He cut pieces out of the horse farm for the rest of his children. Harriet teamed up with Jack Cole to put the tax people on us. They wanted to run us out. Hub put a stop to it. Harriet and Calvin can't touch Bratcher Patch, even if Hub dies."

"Calvin won't be touching anything. He's six feet under with a noose around his neck," Lottie replied, with the news of Hub's kindness towards his children still sinking in.

Martha Ann giggled. So giddy to have Avery home, she couldn't contain her joy. It spilled out when she said, "And John Simpson started talking, Lottie. Miracles are happening all around us."

Lottie rode for a minute or two, trying to process all that she had just been told. She asked, "James, is all this true?"

"Yes, Lottie. It was Pa and Avery that shot at Tiller. It was Pa that Martha Ann saw in the shadows. He's been watching out for us all along."

"That answers that question, "I thought it was Patrice and Patrick Cole," Lottie said.

Avery had more information. "The Cole twins have been to Bullhead to see Hub. He keeps supplies for them and the people they help in the swamp. It was them what told Hub about what Jack and Harriet were up to."

"I knew they were involved in something. I just couldn't figure out what," Lottie said.

"I went back in the swamp with them. You'd be real lost if you didn't follow someone that knew the way. Patrick said his grandfather told him the Tuscarora hid in the swamp for years. There's a whole village back in there."

Martha Ann chimed in, "So, we're going to get Pa and nurse him back to health. Avery said he was shot through the shoulder, the bullet is out, and he just needs some root medicine to beat back the fever."

James added to Martha Ann's news, "Pa is coming to live with Ma like he was meant to all along. He took Harriet over to Delphia's place and put her out after he found out what she and Jack were up to."

"Why does he have to live at the Patch?" Lottie asked, still not ready to forgive and forget.

James looked up at Lottie. Even standing in the wagon, he wasn't as tall as she was on the back of Big John.

"Lott, it ain't hit you yet, but love is a force to be reckoned with. Our Pa and Ma haven't had it easy, but they never stopped loving each other from the time they were younger than you are now. When you find love, it will turn you inside out, and you'll do whatever it takes to keep it."

"But he left her, married Harriet, and then just used Ma when he could get away to see her. That isn't love, James."

"Lottie, after I was born, Pa's father threatened to send Ma to Georgia, if Hub didn't marry Harriet. He wanted that Lane land, and he used his son to get it."

"He couldn't do that. Ma is free and white. He didn't own her."

James hesitated for a second and then said, "Yes, Lottie, he did. Her Pa signed a contract for indenture with Brantley Edwards for the land my house sits on. She wasn't free of that contract until after Jefferson was born."

Lottie stared straight ahead. She couldn't process all the new information.

John Simpson quietly said, "I know it will take a miracle to bury all that hate you have for your Pa, Lott, but let it rest. Of all Hub Edwards's children, he always thought you were the most like him.

He loves you more because of your pride and determination to despise him."

"How do you know that, John Simpson?" Lottie asked.

"Because he used to come walk with me in the dark at night. He talked, and I listened."

James elbowed John Simpson. "Jane thought you were running around on her. You should tell her the truth."

Lottie saw John Simpson smile for the first time since he came home, as he replied, "I will." He looked up at Lottie. "Don't carry that burden of hate anymore. The war is over, on all fronts."

Lottie thought for a few more minutes. Everyone else stayed quiet. She could feel eyes on her, waiting to see what she would say or do next. The thing was, Lottie didn't know either. She could go on hating Hub or give up and take what life had dealt her.

Lottie figured this was what her Ma meant when she said, "It's hard for folks to live up to your expectations of them, Charlotte Bratcher. Everyone in this world is flawed, even you. You'll be a lonely old woman if you continue to expect folks to be perfect."

Lottie looked down at James, her decision made. "I think Jefferson and the twins took Hub to Goldsborough. That was the plan when I left. Go home. You can't get into town, but I can."

Martha Ann piped up from the back of the wagon, "Jefferson is home too? Praise Jesus. See, Lottie, miracles are happening all around us."

Chapter Twenty-Four

Relative Revelations

"Miss Patrice and Mr. Patrick have retired to their chambers for the evening."

"You must be Herman. I'm a friend of the Coles. I was here last night. I'm looking for my brother. I didn't find him at the hospital. I thought he might be here."

"I wouldn't know about that, miss."

"It's fine, Herman. Please, come in, Lottie," Patrice said, as she floated down the stairs in a pure white linen nightgown.

Lottie, struck dumb by Patrice's graceful descent, exhaled audibly. She suspected Herman heard her.

Herman smiled and opened the door wider. "Come in, miss. Would you like me to retire your horse to the stable?"

"I don't know if I'll be staying," Lottie answered. "Patrice, do you know where Jefferson is?"

"Yes, I do," Patrice answered and then addressed Herman, "Would you be so kind as to tend to Miss Bratcher's horse? She'll be in for the evening."

The scent of roses arrived before Patrice. It was never overpowering, just a hint of roses in the air. It was an elixir Lottie could not resist. Patrice presumed that Lottie would stay without asking. She was correct in her assessment of the spell she cast over Lottie.

"Thank you," Lottie said to Herman, "but I better walk him back there. He's had a rough couple of days."

"Haven't we all," Patrice said. "I'll wait for you upstairs then."

Herman led Lottie around to the stable, where two Yankee guards stood watch over the horses inside. Lottie pulled Big John's tack off and rubbed him down. She made sure the water bucket was full and filled the feed trough in his stall with fresh hay and a portion of oats, courtesy of the Yankee's staying in the house.

"Eat your fill, big man. Don't you break out of here and go for a wander. Behave yourself and get some rest." She hugged his neck. "Thank you, brother."

Big John snorted and bobbed his head.

"Good boy. Rest now."

Lottie noted Uncle William's mare in the stall at the end. The twin's bays stood between the mare and Big John. Several other horses were in the stalls on the other side of the stable.

"This eight-stall stable is large for a house in town," Lottie said to Herman, who had stayed close with her.

"Mrs. Cane had a lot of guests. She wanted their horses to feel welcome to, she said. God rest her soul."

"I think I would have liked Mrs. Cane."

"Oh, Miss Patrice is some like her. She has her grandmother's spirit in her for sure."

Herman chuckled and then led Lottie back into the house and escorted her to Patrice's bedroom door.

"Good night, miss," he said with a bow.

"Thank you, Herman."

Lottie reached to knock on the door, but it flew open. Patrice stepped aside, allowing Lottie to enter and then closed and locked the door behind her.

"You smell like a stable boy," Patrice said.

"Do you go about smelling stable boys, Miss Patrice?" Lottie asked playfully.

"Not if I can avoid such occasions. Give me that cape and your other clothing. There is a basin on the dresser with soap and fresh water. No bath tonight, I'm afraid."

"You said you knew where Jefferson is. Is he here?"

"All in good time, Miss Bratcher. First, let us deal with the horse in the room. Your clothing, remove it, please."

Lottie undressed without the lesson in passion from last night. They were already comfortable with each other. It felt odd to be so at ease with Patrice, after so many years of avoiding her. But all the fight had gone out of Lottie. She was exhausted, both physically and emotionally. Lottie desperately wanted the whirlwind of the last twenty-four hours to spin itself out and let her rest.

Patrice took Lottie's clothes and left the room. Lottie washed and slipped into the nightgown Patrice had laid out for her. It wasn't the elegant embroidered gown Patrice was wearing, but it was clean and soft and smelled like roses. Lottie breathed in the scent as she pulled the fabric over her head.

Patrice reappeared with a platter of sliced ham and freshly baked biscuits. She smiled at Lottie, "I thought you might be hungry."

"I am near starved," Lottie said, as Patrice put the platter on the table by the chaise lounge.

Patrice sat on the chaise and patted the seat beside her. "Quite a few perks come with having a home the Yankees want to occupy. I truly don't mind having them here. We are safer now than before they arrived. They have been nothing but gentlemen, and they share their bounty. Those old biddies at the hospital complain out of one side of their mouths and stuff the other side with eggs and bacon provided by the officers in their homes."

"You don't seem the least bit surprised to see me," Lottie said.

"Jefferson said you'd be along. He said you were pigheaded, but you loved Hub Edwards, or you wouldn't hate him so much. I believe this may be a pattern with you."

Lottie smiled sheepishly, but her mouth was full of ham and biscuit. It wasn't until the first bite that she remembered she had not eaten all day. She stuffed her mouth like a ravenous child and tried not to chew like a cow.

"Let me fetch some water," Patrice said and floated across the room. "You were famished."

When Patrice moved quickly, the linen pressed against her body. Lottie noted her return down to the minutest detail. Her mind stripped the cloth from Patrice's skin. Lottie knew full well what lay beneath the fancy thin cotton. She swallowed hard and accepted the glass of water gratefully.

"Thank you."

185

"I take it you saw Hub at the hospital and have learned all the details of what has come to pass."

Finally able to speak after consuming the water, Lottie replied, "He was asleep, but the doctor said he would probably recover." She returned the now empty water glass to Patrice, who placed it on the table. Lottie continued, "Medicine Mary said she had seen far worse get up and walk out a few days after she plastered them with healing herbs. The bullet went clean through and hit no bone. He was fortunate."

"Hub told us Gabriel shot him in the shoulder, before he took the bullet to the forehead. He followed Hub in the back door. Jack sent his own son in there to murder someone. Your Pa thinks Harriet and Jack plotted to kill him after he discovered their plan to take the Patch from you. You do know that it isn't going to happen. He gave you the land outright."

"I ran into James and half my family. They explained everything, including what you and Patrick have been up to. Now, I know why you knew so much."

"I couldn't tell you, Lottie. It would have put you in more danger. You already had a gang of horse thieves after you and a bunch of deserters to take care of."

"I understand. I had to keep secret about Jefferson and the boys in the swamp." Lottie thought for a second and then added, "Neither you or Patrick seemed surprised to see Jefferson."

Patrice grinned. "Your brother didn't stay put in that swamp. He's a bit high-strung, like his sister."

"And you just happen to carry parole papers? Like I told your brother, we'll be bearing each other's secrets from here out. What are you into, Patrice?"

"There are groups of women who organize things. We're working to end the war and stop the bloodletting. I told you I have no side. My enemy is manhood defined by war, a legacy we relive throughout history."

"Why? Why did Jack want that near worthless piece of bottomland?"

"Revenge," Patrice said.

Lottie knew her expression was that of surprise. In her current state of exhaustion, her voice cracked with emotion when she asked, "Revenge for what? How has anyone out at Bratcher Patch ever harmed a rich man like Jack Cole?"

Instead of answering Lottie's question, Patrice pushed a lock of curls from Lottie's forehead. "You are so defenseless when you're tired. I don't think I've ever seen you without a façade of toughness."

"Patrice, I've lived more in the preceding twenty-four hours than I have in the last eighteen years. I don't have any fight left in me. I didn't come here only because I thought Jefferson might be here. I came because I want to crawl into your arms and sleep like I did last night."

Patrice smiled slyly and winked. "Did we sleep?"

Lottie felt her skin blush with heat. "Not very much, but when we did, I...I don't know. I have never felt that still. I'm always so restless. You have a power over me I can't explain. I've avoided you half my life because of how you make me feel and now all I want is to feel how I do when I'm with you."

Patrice leaned closer to Lottie. Her lips found Lottie's waiting, anticipating, craving her touch. When her hand slipped into Lottie's hair and pulled her closer, it wasn't the hungry, passionate kiss from the previous evening. This time it was sweet and long, a slow burn down to Lottie's soul.

Lottie felt the walls melt away, her eyes closed, as she felt the day leave her until all that was left was Patrice, Patrice's lips on hers, their tongues in a slow dance. As the kiss deepened, Patrice leaned back into the corner of the chaise, pulling Lottie with her.

The knock on the door startled them both into sitting position.

"You are not asleep, and you haven't had time to do anything else, so open up," Patrick's slightly drunk voice sounded outside the door.

"Is this a pattern with him?" Lottie asked.

"What we share as twins is an unusually keen sense of what is happening with the other." Patrice rose and walked toward the door. "Even without that ability, I can tell you my brother is nearly as happy as I am at the moment and well into Grandmother's brandy." She smiled over her shoulder at Lottie. "Brace yourself, Lottie. You're about to have your answer as to why Jack Cole wanted revenge on the people of Bratcher Patch."

187

Patrice turned the key in the door, turned the handle, and allowed two intoxicated men into the room. Lottie jumped to her feet when she saw her brother.

"Well, Lott, I guess we're more alike than we thought."

Jefferson Edwards, bathed, shaved, and dressed in one of Patrick's suits, beamed at Lottie. He held a brandy snifter in one hand and a cigar in the other. The arm of the hand holding the cigar was draped over Patrick's shoulder. The smoldering look in Patrick's eyes left no doubt who Jefferson was to him.

It suddenly all came clear to Lottie. "You are the one Jack caught with Patrick. That's why you left. He was going to kill you."

"That is a fact, Lott. Except I was going to kill Jack for what he did to Patrick. It was Pa that sent me away. Said he didn't want me to hang for it."

Lottie sat down on the chaise, too exhausted to have this conversation, but have it they did.

She said, "Well, now, isn't this something. What are we going to do?"

Jefferson left Patrick and walked over to sit beside Lottie. He wrapped an arm around her shoulder and handed her the brandy.

"Tomorrow, we'll worry about the logistics of things," he paused and held his hand out, indicating the Cole twins, who stood arm in arm smiling back, "but tonight we each sleep with angels. Look at them. My God, they are beautiful."

Lottie swallowed a sip of brandy, before she said, "And they smell"—Jefferson joined her—"like roses."

The Daily Standard
Raleigh, N.C.
Monday, June 26, 1865

MARRIED.

In Goldsborough, on the 24th of June, by Rev. Jonah Stancil, at the groom's residence, Mr. PATRICK HENRY COLE to Miss CHARLOTTE BRATCHER, all of this place.

In Goldsborough, on the 24th of June, by Rev. Jonah Stancil, at the bride's residence, Mr. HUBBARD JEFFERSON EDWARDS to Miss PATRICE HENRIETTE COLE, all of this place.

Author Bio

Four-time Lambda Literary Award Finalist in Mystery—
Rainey Nights (2012), *Molly: House on Fire* (2013), *The Rainey Season* (2014), and *Relatively Rainey* (2016)—and 2013 Rainbow Awards First Runner-up for Best Lesbian Novel, *Out on the Panhandle,* author R. E. Bradshaw began publishing in August of 2010. Before beginning a full-time writing career, she worked in professional theatre and also taught at both university and high school levels. A native of North Carolina, the setting for the majority of her novels, Bradshaw now makes her home in Oklahoma. Writing in many genres, from the fun southern romantic romps of the Adventures of Decky and Charlie series to the intensely bone-chilling Rainey Bell Thrillers, R. E. Bradshaw's books offer something for everyone.

Learn more here www.rebradshawbooks.com